A NOTE TO READERS

While the Miltons and Langs are fictional, the turmoil in Boston leading up to the Revolutionary War is not. By the time war broke out, one in every four people in Boston was a British soldier. These soldiers were everywhere—in people's homes, businesses, and public meetinghouses. Whether citizens were Loyalists or Patriots, most of them wished there were far fewer in their town. In spite of all the soldiers, Patriots continued to work secretly for American rights.

D0647235

SISTERS IN TIME

Kate
and the Spies
THE AMERICAN REVOLUTION

JOANN A. GROTE

BARBOUR
PUBLISHING

© 2004 by JoAnn A. Grote

ISBN 1-59310-354-9

All rights reserved. No part of this publication may be reproduced or transmitted for commercial purposes, except for brief quotations in printed reviews, without written permission of the publisher.

Churches and other non-commercial interests may reproduce portions of this book without the express written permission of Barbour Publishing, provided that the text does not exceed 500 words or 5 percent of the entire book, whichever is less, and that the text is not material quoted from another publisher. When reproducing text from this book, include the following credit line: "From *Kate and the Spies,* published by Barbour Publishing, Inc. Used by permission."

All Scripture quotations are taken from the King James Version of the Bible.

Cover design by Lookout Design Group, Inc.

Published by Barbour Publishing, Inc., P.O. Box 719, Uhrichsville, Ohio 44683, www.barbourbooks.com

Our mission is to publish and distribute inspirational products offering exceptional value and biblical encouragement to the masses.

 Member of the
Evangelical Christian
Publishers Association

Printed in the United States of America.
5 4 3 2 1

CONTENTS

1. Mysterious Visitors 7
2. A Wild Tea Party. 14
3. What Happened to Liberty? 23
4. Will Boston Starve? 31
5. Signs of War 39
6. A Spy. 45
7. The Warning 57
8. A Secret Code 63
9. Escape from Boston. 72
10. A Dangerous Mission 80
11. The Deserter 86
12. A Safely Delivered "Package" 93
13. Fighting Friends and a Late-Night Secret 99
14. The Raid 108
15. Danger. 116
16. A Mission of Mercy. 126
17. War!. 132

CHAPTER 1

Mysterious Visitors

Boston, December 16, 1773

"Oof!"

Eleven-year-old Kate Milton braced against the crowd that dragged her and her cousin Colin Lang along. Whistles and yells from merchants, craftsmen, and seamen filled the early night air.

"A Boston tea party tonight!" called a large man beside her. From the smell of him, Kate guessed he was one of Boston's many fishermen.

Kate struggled to keep her footing on the slippery wet stones of Boston's Milk Street. She hung on tightly to Colin's arm, clinging to him for support. Thousands of people filled the streets. She had never seen such a crowd in Boston. She and her cousin had no choice but to go the same way as everyone else. Her heart beat like crazy beneath her wool bodice. She and Colin had wondered for weeks what would happen tonight, and now they were about to find out!

"Where's everyone going?" Kate had to yell to be heard. She tipped her head back, trying to see Colin's face, but he was taller than she was, and his face was turned away as he scanned the crowd. Kate stood on tiptoes and pushed back the gray wool cloak from her blond curls, but she could still only see the backs of the people ahead of them.

"We're headed toward Griffin Wharf at Boston Harbor," Colin shouted. "The tea ships are there."

Kate felt fear settle in her chest like a rock. "Are the people going to hurt the crews? Will they sink the ships?"

"I don't think so," her cousin answered. "People aren't carrying weapons or sticks or stones."

When they reached Griffin Wharf, Kate had to step carefully to keep from tripping on the slippery wooden planks and huge coils of rope. Beneath them, water lapped at the tall wooden poles that held up the dock.

The people filled the wharf to the very end. Judging by the light from tin and wooden lanterns on long wooden torches that people carried, Kate guessed the next wharf was just as crowded.

The *Dartmouth,* one of three ships carrying tea, rose high above them. It tugged at the thick ropes tying it to the pier. The other two tea ships were anchored nearby.

Kate looked at the three ships, dark outlines against the darker sky of early evening. With their sails rolled up, the ships' straight pine masts stood like tall, leafless trees, but the ships themselves were like great winged beasts, poised to swoop into the air. "The ships look like dragons, don't they?" Kate whispered.

Will the ships still be here in the morning? she wondered. *Will the tea?*

At least the rain had stopped. The December chill crept through Griffin Wharf's wet wooden planks, up through the soles of Kate's leather shoes, through the three layers of itchy wool stockings, through the woolen petticoats beneath her gown, and right into her bones. She shivered, yanked her hood over her head again, and wrapped her cloak more tightly around her shoulders.

It's not only the cold that makes me shiver, she thought. *It's fear.*

Fear for Boston. Fear of the unknown. Fear for her older cousin Harrison's life.

The fear had been crawling inside her ever since that day two weeks ago at her uncle's print shop. That was when Harry had told Colin and Kate what might happen and had asked them to help.

They'd been printing handbills, or posters, for the Sons of Liberty. Kate didn't mind helping, but she liked helping her father better. Her father was Dr. Firth Milton, and Kate was fascinated with the thought that he could actually do something to help sick people heal.

As he had talked to them, Harry's eyes, as brown as Colin's, had flashed with excitement. He'd leaned across the huge printing press and told them the plan in a loud whisper. "The law says the *Dartmouth* has to either leave Boston on December sixteenth or unload its tea by then."

"I know." Colin and Kate were hanging up copies of the paper, fresh from the press, to dry. "They've only fourteen days left."

"Mark my words, the tea won't be unloaded or sold here."

Kate frowned. She always felt so powerless in the face of all the events that swirled around her, but Harry sounded as confident as if he had some control over what happened. Harrison was twenty-two, nine years older than Colin. He was an adult, and a man besides, while Kate was only a little girl. Still, what could he or the other men do? "I don't understand," Kate said.

Harry spoke quickly, excitedly. "If the ships are unloaded here, we Patriots will do it ourselves. It will take lots of hands. We need men and boys to help who aren't well known in town." He glanced at Kate. "You'd pass for a boy if you tucked your hair up inside a hat and wore some of Colin's old clothes. We need people to help us who can be trusted not to tell what they do that night—not before and not after.

You're Patriots, the both of you, and I'd trust you with my life."

Pride flooded Kate at her cousin's words, but she still felt uneasy.

"I'm a Patriot, all right," Colin said proudly, "and I'll keep your secret. You can count on us."

Kate nodded silently. What else could she do? She couldn't let Harry down.

Kate knew her father referred to people like Harry as rebels, but she had to admit she liked the word "Patriot" better. Rebel sounded like an enemy of King George III. Patriot sounded like a loyal British citizen, and that's what both Colin and Harry were. And so was she, she supposed.

Harry grinned at the two children. "Then you'll help?"

"I don't know." Kate still wasn't certain about this. "How are you going to unload the tea?"

"We're going to throw the tea into the harbor."

Kate's heart thumped like a drum. "You're going to ruin it?" Her voice rose in a squeak, and Harry waved his hand to shush her. He nodded once, sharply.

"But. . .but that's like stealing!" Kate's chest hurt from the deep breaths she was taking. Surely her cousin wouldn't steal, even to keep the tea out of Boston!

"We'll only do it if we have to. We're trying to get the governor to send the ships away with the tea. If he does, we won't have to toss the tea overboard."

"What if the governor has you arrested for dumping the tea?" Colin asked.

"That's why we need boys that most adults in town won't know. Lots of boys your age are helping. Are you with us?" Harry looked from Colin to Kate.

Kate swallowed. "I can't. It's too much like stealing."

She was relieved when Colin nodded his agreement. Would Harry think they were cowards? Colin and Harry looked alike, and they were both Patriots, but in many ways the two brothers were very different. Harry was always doing exciting things, while Colin was quiet, serious. He thought things through carefully before making decisions. Still, Kate knew how much Colin looked up to his older brother.

"You have to do what you believe is right," Harry said.

Colin let out his breath with relief. Kate knew he had been scared Harry would be angry with him.

"But," Harry continued, "I have to do what I believe is right, too. I know you won't tell anyone what I've told you."

Neither of them had told anyone Harry's secret. Kate would have liked to talk things over with her father, but she knew she couldn't. Her parents were Loyalists, who believed the Patriots should do as Parliament and the king said, even if what they said was wrong. He wouldn't want to get Harry in trouble, but if her father knew Harry's secret, he might think it was his duty to tell the British admiral. Then Harry's friends would be in trouble.

Kate just wanted to go home. She tugged at her cousin's coat sleeve "Let's go."

"We'll never make it through this crowd." Colin's teeth were chattering so hard that Kate could barely understand him. "If only the governor had let the *Dartmouth* leave tonight with her tea, everything would have been fine."

"Why are people making such a fuss about the tea?" Kate asked. "The tax on it is small, and people like tea." She had heard people talk about the tea in her uncle's print shop many times, but she still couldn't really understand why everyone was so upset. When she was with Colin, she called herself a Patriot because he was one—but when she was with her own family, she couldn't help but think that their point of view made sense, too.

"In Britain," Colin explained, "Parliament passed the tea tax law. Older laws say only people who serve us can pass laws taxing us. No one in Parliament serves the Americas."

Kate's gray wool cloak lifted as she shrugged her shoulders. " 'Taxation without representation.' People say that all the time. But the king chose representatives for the American colonies."

"Those men vote the way the king wants, or they lose their jobs. If we elected them, they'd have to vote the way we want."

"Parliament has a right to make laws, even if Americans don't like them." Kate's pointed chin jutted out. Sometimes out of sheer stubbornness, she liked to argue with Colin, trying to make him see the Loyalists' perspective.

As she spoke, the crowd grew suddenly still. Kate looked around, hoping no one had heard her. What was happening? She stretched onto her tiptoes, trying to see above the people. "I hate being short!"

The crowd opened to let a few raggedly dressed boys and men through.

Kate grabbed Colin's arm. "Indians!"

The newcomers were only pretending to be Indians, she realized as they drew closer. Anyone could tell they weren't genuine natives. She could smell the grease and soot they'd used to darken their faces. Swipes of paint brightened some noses. Knit caps hid hair. Feathers were stuck in a few caps. Blankets draped over shoulders.

But it was what they carried that made Kate's heart beat faster: metal things that glittered in the light from the torches and lanterns.

"Axes!" she whispered. "What are they going to do with them?"

No one answered her.

As more "Indians" came, people pressed even closer together to give them room. Kate thought there must be over one hundred of them.

One of the ragged, smelly young men bumped against Kate. The man winked at her and then passed on to join the others.

Kate stared after him, then nudged Colin. Harrison!

CHAPTER 2
A Wild Tea Party

Harry was helping the "Indians" pull one of the other two tea ships up to the wharf. Fear made Kate's stomach feel like it was wrapped around itself as tightly as the thick ropes tying the ships to the wharf were coiled. What was going to happen? Would Harry and the other Patriots dare go through with their plan?

In the moonlight, she could see the harbor was filled with every size and kind of ship and boat, just as it had been all her life. Somewhere out there in the dark harbor, British soldiers were stationed at the fort on Castle Island. Warships were in the harbor, too. She could see the lanterns on the British man-of-war that bobbed only a quarter-mile away. All of Boston knew that the governor had ordered the ships and fort to fire their cannons on the tea ships if they left the harbor with the tea on board.

She yanked on Colin's sleeve again. "Do you think the men-of-war will fire their cannons at these Indians?"

"Of course not. They might hurt innocent people."

Kate crossed her arms. "Those Sons of Liberty," she hissed. "Sons of Trouble, Papa calls them. He says they're nothing but troublemakers, always stirring people up. There must be other ways to get Britain to listen to what people want."

Colin didn't answer. She knew he wouldn't criticize the Sons of

Liberty, even if he might secretly agree with her. After all, his brother, Harry, was a Son of Liberty.

Kate studied the "Indians." Many looked like they might be about her age or a little older. Were any of them Colin's friends?

Five more joined the group. A man who acted like a leader greeted them by saying, "Me know you." The voice sounded familiar. The five repeated the three words. Kate guessed it was a sign, a way the "Indians" would know there wasn't a spy in the group. They didn't sound like Indians, though, and her lip curled. They were like little boys playing a game of make-believe. But she knew there could be serious consequences to this game.

The moonlight rested on the man's face. Kate squinted at him. Was that Paul Revere, the silversmith who stopped at the printing shop to talk with Harry so often? Surely not. Harry had said they wanted people who wouldn't be recognized, and lots of people knew Mr. Revere. Still, the man's voice had sounded like Mr. Revere's.

The "Indians" quietly boarded the three tea ships. Standing close to the *Dartmouth*, Kate heard someone on deck say, "We no hurt your ship, Captain, only the tea. Please bring lanterns."

Was the speaker afraid someone would recognize his voice if he spoke normally? Kate wondered.

In a few minutes, lanterns shone on the three ships' decks. Then came *whack! whack! whack!*—the sound of axes chopping open wooden chests. In the light from the lanterns and the moon, Kate and the crowd watched smashed boxes drop over the ships' sides.

Kate gasped. "They're really doing it! They are throwing the tea into the water! Where are the constables, or the night watchmen, or the marines?"

"I guess they can't get through the crowd," Colin answered. "Maybe they don't know what's happening."

"We were right, Colin," Kate whispered. "I don't care what Harry said. These people are no better than thieves! Why doesn't someone stop them?"

"No one wants trouble, Kate. They just want the tea unloaded tonight like the law says it must be."

"The law doesn't mean it's to be unloaded this way, and you know it!"

Colin shifted his feet uncomfortably. Kate knew that what was happening was illegal. Still, she had to admit that the Patriots had tried to have it sent legally away from Boston first.

She was surprised to see both Loyalists and Patriots watching quietly. Did the Loyalists think, like the Patriots, that destroying the tea was the only thing left to do?

She didn't see any of the Patriot leaders in the crowd. She and Colin had seen Sam Adams, John Hancock, Josiah Quincy, and Dr. Warren earlier at the town meeting at Old South. Was it too dangerous for them to be seen here?

The terrible "game" went on for three hours. The children stood frozen, trapped by the crowd, listening to the whack of axes, the sound of canvas tearing—Kate guessed that was the bags inside the wooden chests, bags meant to keep the tea dry if the chests got wet. The bags wouldn't help now.

Splintered chests splashed as they landed alongside the ships, and the wooden chests bobbed in the moonlight. Spilled tea drifted like seaweed on top of the dark water. She could smell the tea over the strong smell of sea and fish.

Her legs had long ago grown tired, and her feet ached. She leaned on Colin, though she knew he must be tired, too. But she had forgotten about leaving. Something kept her there, as though she needed to bear witness to something important that was unfolding out there in the harbor. No one else left, either.

For a while, she watched nervously for boats of marines to come from the men-of-war. They never came.

When all the tea had been dumped, the "Indians" finally left the ships. They lined up, four in a row. *Just like soldiers,* Kate thought, so tired now that she felt like collapsing. They rested their axes on their shoulders the same way soldiers rested their rifles. Someone played a tune on a fife.

The tea destroyers marched down the wharf toward town. Kate spotted Harry again, and Colin must have seen him, too, because he lunged toward his brother, keeping a tight hold on Kate's hand so they wouldn't lose each other. Colin grinned as he kept up with the "Indians," who were now humming the cheerful tune the fife played, and Kate found that she couldn't help but smile as well. Now that everything was over, she almost wished she and Colin had joined Harry. It couldn't have been so bad after all, since even the Loyalists and British marines hadn't tried to stop it. Surely no one would be arrested. It would have been exciting to be part of it.

The marching men reached the head of Griffin Wharf, where buildings lined the street at the edge of the harbor. Wood squeaked against wood as a window opened. Kate looked up just in time to see a man shove his head out the window above them. Admiral Montague of the British marines! He'd watched the whole thing!

Kate stopped in her tracks so fast that the man behind her ran right into her. She didn't even notice.

"Well, boys," the admiral said, "you've had a nice night for your Indian caper, haven't you? But mind, you've got to pay the fiddler yet."

One of the "Indians" made a cocky reply. The admiral slammed the window closed.

The men started marching again. Kate's thoughts spun as she followed. She wasn't smiling now. The admiral's words made her sick to her stomach with fear. How would the admiral make Harry and the tea raiders "pay the fiddler"?

"We'd best get home, Colin," she said with a sigh. She was suddenly so exhausted that she thought her legs might give out beneath her.

"I didn't realize it was so late," Colin said as they threaded their way through the crowded streets toward Kate's house. "It must be after nine o'clock. I'll walk you home. You shouldn't be on the streets alone this late."

"Mama will be furious I'm still out." Kate sighed again. All she wanted to do was crawl into her bed. She didn't want to have to face an angry mother.

But they were barely through the front door when her mother met them in the hallway. Like Kate, Mama was short with blond hair and blue eyes, but she wasn't slender like her daughter. Usually, Kate felt comforted by her mother's soft shape, but tonight even Mama's white apron and crisp skirts seemed to crackle with rage.

"Where have you been, young lady?" Her eyes flashed as she faced the children.

"We were at the meeting at Old South Meetinghouse. You said I could go, remember?"

"That was early this afternoon. You know you're to be home before dark. Your father is out searching the streets for you."

"But Mama, you can't imagine what happened!"

"I've been imagining all kinds of dreadful things happening to you!"

"I've been with her the whole time, Aunt Rosemary," Colin spoke up.

"Humph! There are things a boy of thirteen like yourself can't protect her from." Mama wrapped her shawl closer about her shoulders. "I shouldn't have allowed you out of the house today at all, Kate. With the Patriots in such a vile mood over the tea ships and the crowds in the streets—why, I wouldn't be surprised if we ended up with another Boston Massacre."

"Oh, no, Mama!" Kate said eagerly. "The British marines didn't do anything to stop the Indians!"

"Indians?" Mama's hand flew to her throat.

"Not true Indians," Kate assured her quickly.

Mrs. Milton shook her head. "I don't know what you are talking about, child. Colin, you'd best get home. Take a lantern with you. Honestly, out on the streets without even a lantern, among the angry crowds. You both should have known better."

"Yes, Aunt Rosemary," Colin murmured, moving past her into the parlor to light a candle for the lantern at the fireplace.

"Don't think you're going to get by without being punished for this," Mama was saying to Kate as Colin slipped out the door.

"But let me tell you about the tea and the Indians," Kate said as the door closed behind Colin.

She knew Mama had been worried, but she didn't understand why being worried always made parents angry. As she listened to her mother scold, Kate wondered how things were going for Colin. At least she didn't have a room full of people listening to her mother reprimand her. Colin would have his older sisters, Isabel, age fifteen, and Susanna, age twenty, as well as Harrison's wife, Eliza, all pretending not to listen to Aunt Jane's shrill voice while they worked on their fancy needlework. Harrison and Eliza's six-month-old baby, Paul, would be asleep in a wooden cradle beside the hearth, and Kate wished she could be there, if only so she could scoop up the round little baby boy and cuddle him in her arms.

Somehow, it helped to imagine Colin's family now, instead of paying too much attention to the anger in her mother's voice. Colin's mother was tall and lean like her brother, Kate's father. She had red hair like her Irish mother. Right now, Kate was pretty sure her aunt's green eyes were stormy.

"I'm sorry, Mama," Kate said, pulling her mind back to her own home, "but we just forgot about the time. We wanted to see what happened, and the crowd was so thick—"

"Go to your room, Katherine Milton," her mother snapped. "I don't want to hear your excuses."

With tears burning her eyes, Kate made her way up to her room. At least she could go to bed now. But she would have liked some supper first.

The next day when she saw Colin, she asked him how things had gone at his house the night before. "Was your mother as angry as mine was?"

Colin grimaced. "More. But she was interrupted before she could really get going."

Kate raised her eyebrows, waiting for her cousin to explain, and Colin grinned. "You see, this strange 'Indian' suddenly came through our back door."

"You mean Harry?. . ."

Colin nodded. "Mother didn't even recognize him until he said,

'It's me, Mother.' And then she wanted to know why he was dressed like that—and why he smelled like tea leaves!"

"Was she upset?" If Aunt Jane had been angry with Colin for being out late, it seemed to Kate that her aunt should have been even angrier with her older son. But Colin shook his head.

"Father came home then—and everyone forgot about me because Harry was telling about the tea party. Ever since the Boston Massacre, you know how my parents have been more sympathetic toward the Patriot cause. Everyone clapped and laughed at Harry's story."

Kate tried to imagine it. She was fairly certain that even if Mama weren't a Loyalist, she would never laugh and clap if Kate broke the law the way Harry had. But Colin's family was different from hers. That was part of the reason why her cousins fascinated her so much, she supposed.

"And then," Colin continued, "Harry took off his shoe and shook it. He had tea inside it. And Mother laughed even harder and said how your mother would hate to see good tea going to waste like that." Colin smiled at the memory. "Mama said she was proud that Harry had stood up for Englishmen's rights." He sighed and his smile faded. "But then she said how glad she was that I hadn't been involved. She'll never think of me as anything but a little boy." His voice was resentful.

Kate gave him a sympathetic smile. "Well, you are the baby of the family."

Colin made a face. "At least Harry doesn't think I'm a baby. But it's a good thing Mother doesn't know he asked us to help with the tea party. She would have been fuming angry then."

"What did your father say?" Kate asked.

"He warned us all not to tell anyone that Harry was involved."

Colin's face puckered with worry. "The marines and constables didn't arrest anyone last night, but we don't know what might happen later."

Kate gave a little shiver. She couldn't help but remember the admiral's warning: *You've got to pay the fiddler yet.*

CHAPTER 3

What Happened to Liberty?

"King George is making Boston 'pay the fiddler' now," Colin said to Kate early in June.

"He's making all Boston pay, not just those men who threw the tea overboard." Kate's mouth bent in a pout.

The peal of bells drifted over the water. All of the churches in Boston had been ringing their bells for hours. Everyone said it was the worst day in Boston's history.

So many months had passed since the tea party that Kate had hoped the king had forgotten about it. He hadn't. Finally a ship came from England carrying the Boston Port Bill, a law passed by Parliament. It said that until Boston paid for the tea it dumped into the harbor, Boston's port would be closed.

From where they stood on Long Wharf, which ran half a mile into Boston Harbor, Kate could see the British man-of-war that was anchored between Long Wharf and Hancock's Wharf. In all, nine men-of-war were now guarding the harbor from entering ships. No other ships were in the harbor. The warships wouldn't let small boats, barges, or ferries approach Boston by harbor or river. A boat couldn't be rowed from one dock to another.

Boston was built on a peninsula that was almost an island. Only a narrow piece of land, called the Neck, connected it to the rest of

Massachusetts. With the harbor closed, the Neck was the only way in or out of town.

At least no one had been arrested for the tea party. No one knew for certain who most of the "Indians" were—and no one would tell even if they did know—so no one had been arrested. The day after, Paul Revere had left for Philadelphia and New York to let people there know what had happened. Sons of Liberty in those cities had sent word that they thought Boston had done the right thing.

Hardly anyone was working. People wandered about town, angry and unable to believe what was happening. A soft salt breeze cooled the summer day but did nothing to cool people's tempers.

Colin and Kate had joined their families in a prayer service at church before coming to the wharf. Loyalists, Patriots, and people who hadn't chosen sides had been there. Everyone was afraid the port's closing would leave people without jobs.

Kate shoved a blond curl behind her ear, out of the breeze's way. "I've never seen the wharf so quiet. There's none of the usual bustle of unloading and loading ships and clerks running about with their ledgers. And none of Uncle Thomas's merchant ships are in the harbor."

The king thought that when Boston's port closed, the other towns would jump at the chance to take business away from Boston. Instead they'd offered to help Boston. Uncle Thomas was in Salem arranging for his ships to land at Salem's port. His merchandise would have to be shipped over land, which would cost more money and make business more difficult, but it would keep business from stopping altogether.

"Only our enemies' ships are in our harbor," Colin's father had said after the prayer service this morning.

Sparks flew from Dr. Milton's eyes. "The British fleet isn't our enemy. Boston is part of England."

Uncle Jack's brown eyes grew cold. "Since when does England point cannons at its own people?"

"Since Boston's people threw someone else's tea into the harbor." Kate's father stared at his brother-in-law, his mouth hard. "Even Ben Franklin sent word from London that the tea party was illegal. He thinks Boston should pay for the tea."

"Boston's citizens would sooner starve."

"I don't think so. There are lots of Loyalists in town. We don't want to lose business because of what those involved with the tea party did. With the port closed, it won't take long for the rest of Boston to come to its senses and pay for the tea."

"Never!"

Dr. Milton waved an arm toward the shops, countinghouses, and warehouses on the wharf. "Can't you see that these buildings are closed and their windows shuttered? The men are without work. People won't be able to buy food or clothing or your newspapers. How are you going to run your print shop?"

"I've bought a good supply of paper and ink," Uncle Jack answered. "I agree things will be rough if people don't have money to buy newspapers or place advertisements. But there will be news the people need to know, and I aim to print it. I'll say things with fewer words and use less paper."

"And when you run out of ink?" Father asked. Kate waited for her uncle's answer. British law said people in America had to buy all their ink from England.

Uncle Jack crossed his arms. "Then Harry and I will learn to make it ourselves."

Kate stared at her uncle. Could they really do that?

"Boston will get by," Uncle Jack continued. "Sons of Liberty in

New York and Philadelphia have promised to help us."

"How?" Kate's father waved a hand scornfully. "With brave words? The other colonies don't care about us. Do you think they'll give Boston fuel, food, and other supplies?"

Kate remembered the picture of the snake her uncle had printed in the newspaper the previous week. Ben Franklin had drawn it many years ago. The snake was in pieces, each piece representing a different colony. The pieces weren't joined together because the colonies always argued among themselves instead of working together. Beneath the picture, Mr. Franklin had written "Join or Die." He'd said that if the colonies didn't work together, they would be like a snake that was cut up into pieces. They would die.

Was Father right? Kate wondered. Wouldn't the other colonies help Boston?

"Remember what I printed in yesterday's paper?" Uncle Jack asked. "Colonel George Washington threatened to raise one thousand men and force the British troops from Boston."

"You wish to see fighting in our streets?" Her father's face was red from fury.

"No, but I don't wish to give up our rights as English citizens, either, just to keep peace."

Kate leaned close to Colin's ear and whispered, "Our fathers haven't stopped fighting in years. Why can't they be friendly like us? You and I don't always agree, but we don't argue about it."

Her father turned to Colin and Kate. "We'd best get back to the apothecary. A doctor's work doesn't stop because people can't pay him. There may be more work than ever for you, Colin. My other apprentice, Johnny, left Boston with his family. You'll have to take over his duties, too. You can start by weeding the medicine herb garden."

Father's long legs set a brisk pace. In her long skirt and petticoat, Kate couldn't keep up. She was grateful that Colin matched his steps to hers. "I didn't know Johnny was leaving," Colin remarked.

Kate lifted her skirts so they wouldn't be soiled by the puddle they were passing. "He and his family went to Salem. Johnny's father is looking for a job there." Kate's forehead puckered with worry. Johnny's father was a carpenter who worked in the shipyards. The Port Bill had put him out of work. She would miss Johnny, and she knew Colin would, too. Johnny wanted to be a doctor more than anything. What if he never had the chance again? Kate's chest ached for him. She couldn't bear it if Uncle Jack made Colin give up his chance to be a doctor. If only she could have the chance to be a healer, too—but Mama said that midwives could only make a living these days in small villages where no doctor came. No daughter of hers, Mama insisted, was going to end up in the backwoods.

Kate sighed. When Kate was much younger, her mother had taught her to read and write—but now that Kate was older, Mama couldn't understand why Kate would want to continue to study and learn. After all, Mama said, a girl only needed to be able to read the Bible and do enough writing and arithmetic to keep house. The big medical books in Father's library fascinated Kate, but Mama said it was a waste of time for Kate to be always poking her nose into the thick books. Mama didn't understand how Kate felt about healing. All Mama wanted was for Kate to grow up and get married to some well-off young man.

Kate noticed that many of the houses they passed were empty. Shops were empty and dark, too. They gave her an eerie feeling. Families leaving town passed them with carts and arms piled high with belongings.

Kate's eyebrows scrunched together. "Johnny's father said the people who stay in Boston are going to starve. Do you think we're going to st—starve?"

"Of course not," Colin said stoutly. "Didn't you hear Father say the other colonies will help us?"

But would they? Goose bumps ran up Kate's arms. Who was right—Father or Uncle Jack?

Hours later at the apothecary, Kate watched while Colin held a small marble bowl in one hand and a marble pestle in the other, grinding soft yellow primrose flower petals into powder. Father wanted them for a patient, and Kate knew the primrose would help the woman's painful hands. The flower's gentle smell filled the air.

The woman had barely left before off-key singing came through the open door:

> *"Rally, Mohawks! Bring out your axes,*
> *and tell King George we'll pay no taxes*
> *on his foreign tea!"*

Father grunted. "You'd think people would be sick of that song about the tea party."

Kate grinned. She kind of liked the song's cheery tune, but she knew it got under the skin of Loyalists like her father.

Kate watched as Colin took his journal from the open shelves, where he always kept it handy. The shelves were filled with white jars. Blue letters told what herbs each held. Kate liked the way the apothecary always smelled of dried flowers and herbs. Drawers below the shelves held roots and barks for medicines and curved saws for surgery.

Colin's quill pen tip scratched across the page as he wrote down what his uncle had told the woman about the primrose. Colin had been an apprentice for almost three years now, and Kate tried hard not to be too jealous of him.

Her father smiled down at his nephew. "I'm glad you like to learn. You're the best apprentice I've ever had."

She watched Colin's cheeks turn pink with pride. "I don't want to forget how to treat all the different sicknesses when I'm a doctor."

"You'll have books to help you remember, like this new one you bought at Henry Knox's bookshop down the street." Her father lifted a thick book bound in brown leather with gold letters.

"I–I want to get a degree from a medical school, too." Colin held his breath. Kate knew it was his greatest dream to get a university degree. He'd never told anyone but her.

Her father shook his head. "You don't need to go to a university to be a doctor. Most doctors learn only through apprenticeship and reading, as you're learning."

"I know, sir, but I want to be the best doctor possible. I want to know everything I can to help my patients."

Father smiled. "Have you decided which university you want to go to?" The tone of his voice told Kate he wasn't taking Colin seriously.

"Either Philadelphia or King's College in New York. They're the only medical schools in the American colonies." Colin's voice was determined.

"Well—"

Crash!

All three of them spun toward the door. Kate's friend, Sarah, leaned against it. Wrapped in her apron, she carried a small tan dog with a black nose and a black tip on its long, skinny tail.

"Liberty!" Kate cried. "What happened to my dog?"

CHAPTER 4
Will Boston Starve?

The lilac dress Sarah wore was covered with dirt. The ties of her white linen scarf had slid up under one ear. She sounded as though she had been running.

"Put Liberty on the counter," Father said.

Kate could see that Sarah was handling the dog gently, but Liberty still whimpered. She ran a hand lightly over the dog's short fur, and her heart ached for her little friend. "It's okay, boy," she soothed.

"It's his right front leg." Sarah was still trying to catch her breath. "He can't walk on it."

Kate's father took the leg carefully between his hands. Liberty yelped and tried to sit up. Kate put her hands on both sides of Liberty's head. "Shh, Liberty."

While her father ran his fingers lightly over the rest of Liberty's body, looking for other injuries, Kate looked at Sarah. "What happened? Was he hit by a carriage?"

Tears pooled in Sarah's blue eyes, but they couldn't hide the anger that flashed there. "No. It was some mean Loyalist boys. When the boys heard me call him Liberty, they said he was a nasty Patriot dog. They threw stones at him!"

Anger flashed through Kate. How could anyone be so cruel?

"His leg is broken," her father said.

"I'll set it." Colin glanced up at the doctor. "I mean, if you don't mind, sir."

"You certainly know how to handle a broken leg by now. I'll get some bandages and wood for a splint." Kate's father started for the small room at the back where wood was stored.

Sarah's blue eyes sparkled above her freckled nose, and her dark brown hair waved over her shoulders. "I yelled at the boys to stop. They called me awful names and kept throwing stones at poor Liberty."

"How did you get Liberty away?" Kate asked.

Sarah shrugged. "I ran into the middle of them and picked up Liberty in my apron."

Colin looked impressed. "Did you get hit by any stones?"

"A couple."

Dr. Milton gently grasped Sarah's shoulders. "Were you hurt?"

Sarah winced. "Not much." She rubbed a dirty spot at the top of one arm. "I think I might have a black and blue spot here." Her hand went to her head and gingerly explored a spot there.

Dr. Milton pushed her scarf back. "Sarah, there's a lump here as large as a goose egg!"

Sarah shrugged again. "Well, I haven't a broken leg like Liberty."

"You could have been hurt badly," Dr. Milton said. "What if a rock had hit you in the face?"

"It didn't. Anyway, I couldn't let them keep hurting Liberty!" She looked up at Dr. Milton. "Please don't tell my parents, though," she pleaded. "I'm really fine."

Dr. Milton shook his head. "I don't know, Sarah. You seem to be all right, but your mother should probably keep an eye on you this evening. I'd hate to see you punished, though, for protecting our dog."

"It's those stupid Loyalist boys who should be punished," Sarah stormed. "Just shows how awful Loyalists are."

Kate laughed and propped her hands on her hips. "My family is Loyalist, remember?"

"I forgot."

Kate giggled when Sarah blushed.

Kate's father started back toward the wood room. "We'd best set Liberty's leg. Go and clean up, Sarah, before you go home. Maybe your mother won't be as upset if you don't look as though you just came through a battle."

Kate remembered the way Mama had been the night she came home late after the tea party. She realized her father must understand that the more worried a mother felt, the angrier she was apt to be.

Kate put her hand on her friend's arm. "Sarah, thank you. You're a good friend and a brave one."

Sarah grinned. "So are you. Even if your family is Loyalist."

Kate knew Sarah and her family were strong Patriots. Her father was even more outspoken about Englishmen's rights than Uncle Jack and Harrison were. She was glad that Father never seemed to hold that against Sarah.

Kate smiled and stroked Liberty's head. "I'm just glad Liberty wasn't hurt any worse."

Liberty tried to lick her hand. Kate didn't know what she would have done if Sarah hadn't saved the little dog from the cruel boys. How could people act so mean? She hated the angry feelings that were swirling through Boston these days, driving people apart.

A month later, shades of pink and orange cast by the rising sun were fading from the sky over Boston's streets and harbor as Colin, Susanna, and Kate hurried down the cobbled, narrow street toward the common. Two- and three-story brick houses hugged the street's edge on either side of them. The homes and shops were built so close their walls touched. Smoke from breakfast fires and craftsmen's fires filled the air.

The young people leaped into a nearby doorway to let a farmer and his creaking, two-wheeled cart pass. Colin grinned and pointed. "Look at the turkey." The bird sat in the cart atop a basket of turnips. It turned its head this way and that and gobbled constantly. "At least farmers can still get into Boston over the Neck to sell their food, even if nothing can come by boat or ferry."

Kate's smile died. "Farmers come to the market, but people aren't buying much. People don't have much money. Sarah's father is a carpenter. He hasn't had any work since the harbor closed."

Many of her father's patients hadn't paid the doctor, either. These days, some people made less money in a month than they used to make in a day.

"Many farmers sell most of their vegetables, flour, and meat to the soldiers and marines," Susanna said. "The redcoats won't starve. Britain sends ships with food for them."

Kate sighed. "Father says things will get worse after harvest is over."

"Harvest is months away," Colin said. "Surely the blockade will be over by then."

Kate's blue eyes sparkled with hope. "Do you think so?"

"I haven't heard anyone say so," he admitted. "Still, I can't believe the British troops would let people starve. Even some of the Patriots are friendly with the soldiers. Some of the soldiers are courting Boston girls. Why, I've even heard that Lieutenant Colonel Percy breakfasts every day with John Hancock. There's no stronger Patriot than Mr. Hancock! Could the soldiers hurt the townspeople when they are so friendly with us?"

"I hope you're right." Kate sighed.

Susanna rested her arm along Kate's shoulders and smiled. "Our heavenly Father will look out for us, you'll see."

"I hope He looks out for us better than the other colonies have," Kate said. "They promised to help us, but they haven't yet." Fear squiggled down her spine. Maybe Father was right and the other colonies weren't going to help Boston.

Before they reached the common, they heard the silver bugles calling the redcoats to drill. The day after the harbor was closed, a regiment of British troops had set up camp on the common. Now four regiments were camped there and two groups of artillery with cannons. Cannons on the common, threatening Boston's own people! In the harbor, men-of-war pointed more cannons at the town. A year ago, Kate would never have thought such a thing could happen.

Still, part of her couldn't help but find it exciting to have the streets, shops, and common filled with soldiers in the bright red uniforms that made people call them "lobsterbacks" and "redcoats." When she watched them drill, a thrill ran through her. She didn't tell anyone, though. She was ashamed to feel that way, no matter what her family believed about the soldiers. Lately, Kate felt torn between Patriots and Loyalists. When she was with Mama and Father, she felt like a Loyalist—but when she was with Sarah or Colin and his family, she felt like a Patriot. Which side was right? Was God on one side and not the other? Or could both sides possibly be right? It was all so confusing that it made her head ache sometimes.

Tents and red-and-white uniforms splashed color across the common's grassy slopes. Soldiers were smothering the fires where they'd cooked their breakfast. Kate could still smell the meat and eggs they'd cooked. Some soldiers were readying horses for the officers. Others were grabbing muskets from where they'd been stacked in a circle and rushing to line up for drill. Men and boys from Boston stood in groups, watching. With the port closed, many had time to watch instead of work.

Kate stopped near a bay-colored horse with a black mane and tail. She ran a hand over the horse's shoulder. It turned its head and sniffed Kate's hand.

"What are you looking at, lass?"

Kate's head jerked toward the tall officer beside the horse. Like all officers, he wore a powdered white wig that curled tightly at his ears and tied in a club in back. His black eyebrows showed his hair's true color.

Kate swallowed the lump in her throat. "I–I was just looking at the fine horse, sir."

"Maybe you were thinking of stealing her. You and your young friends here." He scowled at Colin and Susanna.

"No, sir! We wouldn't!"

The officer crossed his arms and looked up and down at the three young people. "I suppose you're all Patriot rebel brats."

Colin's hand balled into a fist. "I'm a—" He stopped short. Kate knew he wanted to say he was a Patriot and proud of it. But Uncle Jack and Harrison had warned all the family to be careful what they said around the soldiers. The Patriot leaders didn't want to anger the troops. "I'm an English citizen," Colin finished lamely.

The officer snorted. "Not a loyal one, I'll bet."

Susanna's fists perched on her hips. Long red curls slipped over the shoulder of her yellow muslin gown. "You needn't speak to him that way. Have British officers no manners?"

"It isn't wise for the town's children to be fooling with an officer's horse, miss." The officer stared boldly at her.

"Is there a problem here, Lieutenant Rand?" Kate turned toward the calm, sure voice. Another officer had stepped up beside them.

Lieutenant Rand straightened. "Just speaking with some of the locals."

"I'm Lieutenant John Andrews." The new officer's friendly, blue-eyed gaze swept over them. "I'm honored to make your acquaintance." Removing his two-cornered black hat, he bowed from the waist. "Have you come to see the troops?"

"No, sir," Colin answered. "We brought medicine for the regiment's doctor."

A frown settled above the blue eyes. "That's a strange delivery, isn't it?"

"I'm Colin Lang, Dr. Firth Milton's apprentice. This is my sister, Susanna, and Dr. Milton's daughter, Kate. Your regiment's doctor sent a soldier to Dr. Milton saying he needed certain herbs. I've brought them for him, but I don't know where to find him."

"The doctor's tent is over there." Lieutenant Andrews pointed to the top of a grassy knoll where a tent was pitched beneath a tall oak. "If I might suggest, it would be best if you young ladies didn't come near the soldiers' camps without a male escort."

Colin stepped between the officer and Susanna. "That's why I'm with them."

Surprise widened Lieutenant Andrews's eyes. Kate waited for him to say that Colin was only a boy. Instead he nodded and shook hands with Colin. "Of course. How wise of you." With another bow to Susanna and Kate, he left.

"He's awfully nice, isn't he?" Kate stared after him.

"He's a British officer. The reason he's in Boston isn't nice at all," Colin reminded her.

Kate smiled hopefully. "Maybe all these soldiers will make Boston pay for the tea, and then everything will go back to the way it used to be."

"Girls!" Colin exclaimed in disgust. "You think there's an easy answer for everything." He stalked toward the doctor's tent, and Kate hurried to catch up with him. She didn't care what Colin said. She was certain that Lieutenant Andrews could make things right again in Boston if he only had the chance.

But then Kate thought of Harry and Uncle Jack and Sarah's father. Men like them were so angry. She sighed. Colin was right after all. There was no easy answer.

When the young people headed back toward town, the streets were filled with more families piling carts with everything they owned and leaving Boston. Kate knew they were afraid there'd be fighting with troops in Boston. Many more troops were on their way.

"Colin! Susanna! Kate!"

They turned to see Harrison running toward them, his tricorn hat in one hand. "Great news!" He stopped beside them, panting and grinning.

"What is it?" Colin asked.

"Rice! South Carolina's sent two hundred barrels of rice. The rice is coming across the Neck now. And Carolina's promised to send eight hundred more barrels." Harry whipped his hat in the air. "They're uniting! The colonies are uniting for Boston!"

CHAPTER 5
Signs of War

To the surprise of the Loyalists and redcoats, gifts poured in over the Neck. The other colonies sent rice, meal, flour, rye, bread, codfish, cattle, and money. A farmer from Connecticut brought an entire flock of sheep.

Colin and Kate's uncle Thomas was on the town's Gifts Committee, along with some of the colonies' strongest Patriots, Sam and John Adams and Josiah Quincy.

When Uncle Thomas asked Kate to help deliver gifts, she eagerly said yes. It didn't matter whether the people she took the gifts to were Patriots or Loyalists. "No one should go hungry, no matter what he believes," she told Colin.

"Thanks to the other towns and colonies, no one in Boston has gone hungry," Colin said.

Kate's shoulders sagged beneath her yellow and blue calico gown. "If the Patriots would pay for the tea, people wouldn't have to beg the committee for food."

"It's not the Patriots' fault King George is punishing everyone in Boston for what the tea partyers did," Colin said quietly.

Kate sighed. Here it was again, the same old confusion that made her head ache. When she was with Colin, sometimes she thought of herself as a Patriot—and other times, like now, she felt as though she had to defend the Loyalists. Lately, she and her cousin argued more and more, just like their fathers did.

Things were tense all over Boston. The men who were out of work were growing angrier every day. They couldn't buy what their families needed, and since they weren't working, they had nothing to do with their time but gripe about their troubles. The men fished off the empty, quiet wharves and complained about the king. They were certain the king was wrong and the Patriots were right. Many people who didn't know whether to be Loyalists or Patriots before the tea party were now becoming Patriots. But not Kate's parents. They were still loyal to England.

Not everything was bleak, though. In order to receive the food that the other colonies had donated, Bostonians had to volunteer for various projects. Streets were paved, buildings were fixed, docks were cleaned, wharves were repaired, and hundreds worked at the brick-yard on the Neck.

"It's like the town is having a housecleaning!" Kate joked to Colin when she came home from making deliveries one day.

On a day in late August, Kate whistled as she walked home from making her deliveries. She knew Mama wouldn't approve of her whistling—"It's not ladylike!" she'd say—but Kate was feeling happy for a change. She liked the bustle and sounds of the street: a boy beating a drum while calling out his master's wares, wooden cart and wagon wheels rumbling along the pebbles, horses' hooves marking a lazy beat, the creak of the wooden signs above every shop swinging in the breeze.

If only there weren't redcoats everywhere, reminding her that everything had changed.

She stopped in the open door of her uncle's printing shop. Lieutenant Rand was waving a sheet of freshly printed paper and yelling at Uncle Jack, Colin, and Harry. "This is treason!" His face was almost as red as his uniform.

Uncle Jack leaned a hip against the tall, wooden printing press and swung his wire-rimmed spectacles in one hand. Kate wondered how he could be so calm with a British officer screaming at him only a couple feet away. "The handbill only tells what our county leaders said today at their meeting."

Lieutenant Rand threw the handbill down and ground it into the wooden floor planks with the heel of his shiny black boot. "They've all but declared war on England!"

"Lieutenant Rand, what they said is not my problem. With the harbor closed, I'll gladly print items for either Patriots or Loyalists in order to feed my family."

Kate watched wide-eyed as Lieutenant Rand clutched the hilt of the sword that hung at his side. Surely the lieutenant wouldn't draw his sword on her uncle! Kate's heart beat so hard it made her chest hurt.

Lieutenant Rand let go of his sword. His eyes glittered with anger. "Mr. Lang, be very careful what you print from now on."

Kate stepped quickly from the doorway to get out of Lieutenant Rand's way as the officer left. "Why is he so mad?" Her voice sounded very small.

Harry grinned. "The Suffolk County leaders drew up this list because of the Port Bill and Intolerable Acts." He handed Kate a copy of the handbill.

The Intolerable Acts were Boston's latest punishment for the tea party. Parliament called them Regulatory Acts. Patriots called them

Intolerable Acts, because they said no Englishman would tolerate or stand for them.

The Intolerable Acts changed the way Massachusetts was run. Instead of elections, the king and his friends chose people for all the important jobs. Juries were even appointed by the king's friends, so it would be hard for people to get fair trials.

Kate stood in the doorway where there was enough light to read the list. "Suffolk Resolves" was printed in large letters at the top. The most dangerous thing it said was just what had made Lieutenant Rand so angry: that Massachusetts's army should train and be ready to fight to keep the rights the king and Parliament wanted to take away.

Fear slid through Kate in an icy wave. "Are the Patriots declaring war on England?"

"No." Harry's brown eyes were serious. "But we need to be ready to protect ourselves."

"We could use your help, children," Uncle Jack said to Kate and Colin. "Paul Revere is waiting for us to finish these handbills. He'll take them to the Continental Congress meeting in Philadelphia."

Kate knew the colonies had decided to hold a meeting called the Continental Congress. People from every colony were invited. They wanted to make a plan to convince the king and Parliament to leave Boston alone and give people in America the rights they used to have.

It's like Harry said months ago, Kate thought. The king meant to hurt Boston by closing the harbor. Instead the Lord was using Boston's trouble for something good, to get the colonies to work together. *Maybe,* she thought, *things will turn out all right in the end after all.*

She watched while Colin put on a leather apron to protect his linen shirt and brown cotton breeches. Kate wet the big pieces of paper, and Colin inked the type with ink-soaked balls of wool and leather. Uncle Jack and Harry took turns swinging the large wooden handle to work the press, and Kate hung up the paper to dry when it came off the press. Before they finished, they had to light candles and lanterns to see.

Kate was thinking as she worked, trying to decide if she was really a Patriot or a Loyalist. It felt good to work hard with her uncle and her cousins. She was glad she could help. Did that mean she was a Patriot?

Mr. Revere arrived as Harry hung up the last handbill. His dark eyes twinkled in his ruddy face. "It looks like you've been helping with the handbills, Colin. We shall make a Son of Liberty of you yet."

Colin grinned, and Kate knew how proud he must feel. She wished Mr. Revere would notice her, too, but men never seemed to pay much attention to little girls.

"I wish I could be with you in Philadelphia, Paul, to hear what the Continental Congress thinks of the handbill," Uncle Jack said, removing his apron.

Harry agreed eagerly. "I wonder if they'll dare say they feel as we do about the army."

"You may be sure I'll let you know." Mr. Revere held out a sheet of copper to Colin's father. "Here's the engraving I promised you."

Uncle Jack put on his wire glasses. He held the metal near a tin and glass lantern to check the picture the silversmith had carved into the copper. "Perfect. I'll use it in the next copy of the *Boston Observer.*"

Mr. Revere picked up some handbills and started for the door. His boots jingled. Kate saw his spurs made the sound.

"Are you leaving tonight?" Harry asked.

Kate knew Sam Adams had set up a system of post riders to carry news between towns and colonies. It was called the Committee of Correspondence. Paul Revere often rode for them.

Mr. Revere said, "The congress begins in only nine days. The trip to Philadelphia often takes twice that long. I've a strong horse, but I'll have a hard ride."

Kate, Colin, and Harry watched from the doorway while Uncle Jack walked with Paul Revere to his horse, which was tied to a post in front of the shop. Kate remembered Mr. Revere's copper engraving. "What is the picture he made, Harry?"

"It shows how to make saltpeter. If war comes, the Patriots will need saltpeter to make ammunition. We won't be able to buy it from England."

War! The word never went away. A shiver ran through Kate. "I thought the Patriots didn't want war. I thought we just wanted things back the way they were."

Harry nodded. "So we do. But we can't always have what we want without a fight. We need to be ready, just in case."

Kate remembered how angry Lieutenant Rand had been earlier that day, how quickly he'd grabbed for his sword. It wouldn't take very much for a few angry men on either side to start a fight like the Boston Massacre four years ago.

But after the massacre, the people of Boston had been able to make peace again. This time if there was a riot and one side began shooting, would the people be able to keep peace—or would there be war?

CHAPTER 6

A Spy

Colin, Kate, and Liberty hurried along the road to the Neck on a cool September day. Sarah's father was helping build a wall there for General Gage, and they wanted to see it. With the harbor closed, there wasn't much else to watch in Boston these days, except soldiers.

A family that looked tired after walking a long way scuffed along carrying bundles and leaning on walking sticks. They were headed toward Boston.

"Another Loyalist family," Kate said. "If we didn't live in Boston, my family might have been forced to leave our home as well."

She couldn't keep the anger and pain from her voice. Patriots in towns other than Boston were mad at the Loyalists for the punishments King George and Parliament were forcing on Boston. Patriots were threatening Loyalists, chasing them from their homes. The Loyalists had nowhere to go but Boston.

"I guess the Loyalists know the redcoats here will keep them safe," Colin said. "How are things going with the Loyalist family from Concord that moved into your house last week?"

"I hate sharing our home with them." Kate kicked at a stone and almost tripped over the petticoat beneath her pink skirt. "Esther—she's my age—shares my bed. She won't play with Sarah because Sarah is a Patriot. Sarah is furious."

"Maybe she thinks you feel the same way as Esther. Sometimes I don't know what you believe, Kate."

"Why does it have to matter?" Kate stamped her foot in frustration. "Sarah's my best friend. She's much nicer than Esther. And you're my cousin. Why should anything like Patriots and Loyalists come between us?" She stuck out her lip, tired with the way everything had changed lately. "There's lots more work with Esther's family, too," she complained.

"Doesn't Esther's mother tell her to help with the chores?"

"Esther and her mother spend all their time saying how terrible the Patriots are and eating our food. Today Esther complained that we hadn't more sweets. With the price of sugar and molasses, we can't afford many sweets."

"She sounds spoiled."

"Mama says not to speak badly of her." Kate sighed. "It must have been awful to be forced out of their home. They only had time to pack a few clothes. I truly am sorry for her."

Life was so confusing lately. Yesterday, she had asked her father why he continued to treat patients who he knew were Patriots, when he didn't believe in their cause. He had looked upset that she would even ask the question.

"A doctor treats everyone, Kate. Regardless of what people believe or what they've done or how much money they have. . .or anything else. You should know that." He sighed. "Besides, each man has to make up his mind for himself about whether to be a Loyalist or a Patriot. I can't force my beliefs on anyone."

Then why do you always argue so much with Uncle Jack? Kate wanted to ask.

But she kept thinking about what Father had said: *Each man has to make up his mind for himself.* She wasn't a man, of course—and how could she make up her mind when she felt so confused?

They reached a small rise in the road, and she saw that soldiers and workmen covered the Neck in front of them. Some were working, others watched. A few days after Paul Revere left for Philadelphia, General Gage had ordered a wall built all the way across the Neck. He called it a fortification because the wall protected the town like the wall of a fort.

It was a cool day, but sweat trickled down Kate's spine beneath her cotton gown. The townspeople couldn't leave Boston by water because of the warships. Now they wouldn't be able to leave by the only road out of Boston if General Gage decided they shouldn't. Seeing the wall and cannons made Kate feel like a prisoner in her own town.

Townsmen were teasing the soldiers. "Can't ye build any better than that?" called one man. "Your wall is no stronger than a beaver dam!" yelled another. "That wall won't protect you. A group of Patriots could blow it down!" called a boy about Colin's age.

Some soldiers ignored them. Others yelled nasty comments back at them. But the townspeople knew the officers wouldn't let the soldiers harm them.

Colin and Kate sat down beneath an oak tree to watch. Workers hauled bricks in two-wheeled wooden carts. Others laid the bricks to make the wall. Sweat glistened off the men's faces. Their shirts were wet with sweat. Officers yelled orders. In the middle of it all, people and carts and donations filed over the Neck along the road into and out of Boston.

Kate's stomach growled. She put a hand over the apron that protected her dress and laughed, embarrassed.

Colin smiled. "Seems everyone's always hungry these days. Thanks to the gifts, at least no one's starving." He pulled two small green apples from his breeches pockets and handed her one. Kate knew the breeches used to belong to Harrison, as had his patched white shirt. Colin had grown so much during the last year that his own clothes no longer fit. "These are from our apple tree."

The children watched a boy a couple years older than Colin push a cart filled with bricks. The boy's red hair was tied back in a club with a piece of leather. He wore a blue farmer's smock that came almost to his knees over his homespun breeches and a black hat with a floppy brim. While they watched, one of the wheels struck a large rock and started to tip.

"Watch out!" Colin jumped up and darted forward.

The boy struggled with the cart's wooden handles, trying to keep the load upright. Before Colin could reach him, the bricks shifted to one side. The cart tipped. Hard clay bricks poured out on top of the boy.

Colin dropped to his knees and frantically pushed bricks off the boy. The lad groaned, trying to sit up.

Other men hurried to help Colin free him. Kate ran and crouched by his side. As the bricks were cleared, Kate fought back a wave of panic at the sight of the boy's leg. The bricks had torn away the knee-high stocking. She could see how badly the leg was hurt.

"We'll have to stop the bleeding," Kate said to Colin.

He nodded and glanced about quickly, then turned to one of the men beside him. "I'm a doctor's apprentice. Is there any drinking water about?"

"I'll get some." The man scurried to get the bucket.

Colin looked up at Kate. "We need something to clean the wound."

She hesitated only a moment, then unpinned the part of the apron that covered the top of her dress and untied the bow in back. Next, she ripped off the square that made up the top of the apron. She tore the apron's ties off and then tore the rest of the apron in half, handing everything to Colin.

The workman returned with the leather water bucket, panting slightly and sloshing water onto the ground in his haste.

The boy clutched Colin's arm. "What—what are yuh goin' to do?" His face was pale as a clamshell and covered with sweat. His hat had fallen off, and his red hair was as damp as his face. Green eyes, huge and frightened, stared up at Colin.

Colin smiled, and Kate knew he was trying to look brave. "I'm going to clean your leg and stop the bleeding so I can see how badly you're hurt."

"It—it hurts somethin' fierce."

Colin nodded. "I know. I'll be as careful as I can, but cleaning it will hurt some more. Can you stand it?"

"I guess I don't have a choice."

"What's your name?"

"Larry. Lawrence Crews. From out Lexington way."

"Well, Larry Crews, if it gets to hurting too much, you just yell at me."

Liberty stuck his nose next to Larry's face and sniffed. Then the dog licked Larry's cheek and laid down beside him, resting his chin on Larry's shoulder. Larry reached out one shaking hand and rested it on Liberty's back. "That's my dog," Kate said. "His leg was hurt awhile back. He understands how you feel."

"Did it heal up good?" Larry asked between clenched teeth as Colin dabbed at his leg with a damp piece of Kate's apron.

"Yes, indeed. He limps a bit, but it doesn't stop him from going wherever he's a mind to."

Kate knelt beside Liberty and started telling Larry about the boys who'd attacked the dog. She was trying to keep Larry's mind off his pain.

The workman who'd fetched the bucket of water held Larry's ankle to keep his leg still while Colin worked. Kate was aware that most of the workmen in the area were standing about, watching.

A minute later, she heard horses' hooves thud against the ground behind her. "What's the problem?" a man's voice asked, and Kate turned her head to see a redcoat officer looming on horseback behind her.

A babble of voices answered him as a number of men all spoke at once. Kate was the one who finally explained. The officer knelt down and laid a hand on Larry's shoulder. "Keep courage, lad. Thank God there was a doctor's apprentice near."

Kate glanced again at the officer. "Lieutenant Andrews!" It was the kind officer they'd met at the common.

The lieutenant nodded. "What can I do to help?" he asked Colin.

"Is there a wagon we could use? I haven't any instruments or medicine with me. We can take him to Dr. Firth Milton's."

Lieutenant Andrews gave sharp orders. Kate admired the way the man quickly arranged for a wagon pulled by two strong horses. The lieutenant ordered hay put in the back of the wagon to make the ride easier for Larry. While the wagon was made ready, Colin tied a clean piece of Kate's apron over the wounded leg with the apron's ties.

Watching Lieutenant Andrews and one of the workmen lift Larry into the wagon, Kate frowned and exchanged glances with Colin. She didn't like the look of that leg. "It will need to be stitched up," Colin muttered in her ear. "I'm afraid some of the nerves and muscles might have been cut by the bricks' sharp edges."

Half an hour later, Larry lay on the counter in the apothecary shop while Kate and Colin watched Dr. Milton examine the leg. "You're right," Kate's father said to Colin with an approving nod, "we'll have to sew it up. One of the muscles is torn but not badly."

Dr. Milton let Colin sew up the badly wounded leg. The doctor held Larry's leg while Colin bent over the leg, concentrating as he used the curved needle. He was sweating from trying so hard to do his work right. Every few minutes he rubbed his forehead against his shoulder so the sweat wouldn't run into his eyes. Kate wished her father would let her help, too. After all, she knew how to sew fine stitches!

Colin was almost through when the bells over the door tinkled cheerfully and Harry entered. He came and stood beside Colin, careful not to block the sunlight, but he didn't say anything.

Taking a deep breath, Colin made the last stitch, tied a knot, and cut the thread.

The doctor smiled. "I couldn't have done better myself."

Larry groaned and opened his eyes. "Is it over?" Dr. Milton had given Larry laudanum to help him endure the pain, but like most patients, Larry had been awake through the stitching. Kate saw Larry was sweating as much as Colin had.

Larry squinted at Harry. "What are you doin' here?"

"Heard about your accident and came to see how you are."

"I'm fine." He nodded toward Colin. "Thanks to this lad." He looked from Colin to Harry and back again. "You two look a lot alike."

They both laughed. People always said Colin and Harry looked alike. It was truer as Colin grew older.

While Dr. Milton, Kate, and Harry talked with Larry, Colin wiped his hands on a rag, then dipped water from a bucket into a basin and washed up.

Dr. Milton wanted Larry to stay in Boston for a couple days so he could keep a watch on Larry's leg. Patients usually stayed at home, but Dr. Milton sometimes let patients from out of town stay on a small bed in his library. He suggested Larry use it.

"You won't be able to do hard labor at the Neck for a while. When the swelling goes down a bit, Colin can use my carriage to take you back to your father's farm," Dr. Milton said.

Kate ran to fetch a blanket and a warm meal for Larry. She often had to help care for patients who stayed in the library, and she was glad for the chance to use her healing skills.

After Kate's father went back to his apothecary's shop, Harry grinned at Larry. "Took your patriotic duty a bit seriously, didn't you?"

Larry managed a small smile, though his lips were still pale from pain. "My load of bricks wasn't dumped on purpose. It was a true accident." Kate thought he looked ashamed. "A British officer was barkin' at some workers, callin' them lazy good-for-nothin's. I was laughin' inside and thinkin' if he only knew what we have in mind for the Neck, he'd be sayin' somethin' worse. Should have been watchin' where I was goin'."

Kate frowned. "What are you two talking about?"

Harry chuckled. "When General Gage needed people to help his soldiers build the wall, the Patriots made sure he got the kind of help we think he needs. The Patriots don't want the wall built. The Patriot workmen work slowly, do sloppy work, and tip over carts filled with supplies, but they make it all look like accidents. They even sunk a barge of bricks."

Kate couldn't believe her ears. "I thought the bargeman ran into an unexpected reef and lost the bricks."

Harrison grinned. "That's what we want people to think. We don't want Gage finding workers who might truly help him."

"Of course," Colin muttered, wiping clean his needle. Kate just pinched her lips together tight. She wasn't sure what she wanted to say, but she knew that whatever it was probably wouldn't have been the right thing.

Lieutenant Andrews stopped by then to check on Larry's leg. Kate thought it was a nice thing for a busy officer to do. She wondered what Lieutenant Andrews would think if he knew why Larry had taken the job on the Neck!

Later, Kate walked with Harry and Colin to the printing shop through the narrow streets. As always, they had to make their way between redcoats. When they reached the shop, Paul Revere was waiting for them.

Harry shook Paul's hand heartily. "Welcome back! Have you brought news of the Continental Congress?"

"That I have." He stepped past Harry, Kate, and Colin, closed the heavy wooden door, and leaned against it. "There are serious things we must talk about."

"Yes." Harry leaned back against the printing press and crossed his arms over his long brown vest. "General Gage didn't like the Suffolk Resolves you took to the Continental Congress. He believes they come too close to declaring war on Britain. On September first, he sent redcoats across the river. They took Charlestown's ammunition."

That had changed everything in Boston, Kate thought. It had made everything worse between the redcoats and Patriots. People in all thirteen colonies were mad as hornets that the redcoats had stolen a town's arms. From the time the first English came to America, towns always had to be ready to protect themselves. No one should take their guns and ammunition! The Patriots were right about that much. Kate settled down on a three-legged stool in the corner of the room. As always, Mr. Revere seemed to barely notice she was there. At least that meant she could listen and think. . .and try to make up her mind whether Harry and Mr. Revere were right.

Harry told Paul Revere about the Charlestown raid. Thousands of Massachusetts men had grabbed their guns and rushed from their villages and farms to help Charlestown. They were too late. The redcoats were already back in Boston.

General Gage was afraid the angry men would take the Neck road into Boston and attack the redcoats. His men had taken four cannons to the Neck to keep them out. Then his men had ruined Boston's cannons so they couldn't be used against the redcoats. He even sent a letter on a ship to England asking the king to send more redcoats to Boston. General Gage was building the wall on the Neck because he was afraid.

"Gage started the wall to keep armed citizens out, but it will also keep redcoats and townspeople in Boston." Paul Revere turned his three-cornered hat in his hands. "People are upset about Charlestown, but maybe it's a blessing to the Patriots."

"How?" Harry asked.

"It showed us that we need to warn the other towns when the troops are getting ready to leave Boston."

"How can we do that?" Colin asked. "The redcoats won't tell Patriots the army's plans."

"That's why we need a group of watchers. Men to watch the army and see when they're getting ready to leave town, men to listen to everything redcoats say for a hint of their plans. Next time Gage plans a raid on a town's gunpowder, we want to get the news to the town first."

Colin shifted uncomfortably. "Can we do that?"

"We must. We'll need a small band of trusted Patriots, about thirty men. Everyone will be sworn to secrecy."

Harry nodded eagerly. "That's a good plan. We can call the group the *Observers.*"

"We'll need a place to meet. What about this shop?"

"No." Harry shook his head. "Redcoat officers are already suspicious about us. They'll be watching the shop."

Colin cleared his throat. "Thirty men meeting in a home or shop would look suspicious, wouldn't they? What if they met at the Green Dragon Tavern? Harry goes there all the time."

Paul Revere rubbed his thumb across his chin. "You're right. No one would think anything of men going to the tavern." He grinned at Colin. "Are you ready to be a Son of Liberty?"

Colin blinked. Kate knew he wasn't sure how to answer. Sometimes Kate suspected her cousin was almost as confused as she was. "I–I already help Harry and Father print things for the Sons of Liberty."

"You can be a far greater help to us if you're willing."

Colin gulped. "I wouldn't hurt anyone or their property. I want to be a doctor. I want to help people, not hurt them."

The silversmith nodded. "I respect you for that. You won't be asked to hurt anyone."

"Then. . ." Colin straightened his shoulders as though he had reached a decision. "I'll be glad to help."

Paul Revere rested a hand on Colin's shoulder. "As a doctor's apprentice, you have good reason to be about Boston. Dr. Milton is a well-known Loyalist. British officers like and trust him. No one would suspect a boy in his shop of spying for the Patriots." For the first time he glanced over at Kate. "You're Dr. Milton's daughter, aren't you, lass? Can we count on your help?"

"S–spying?" Kate's voice was a squeak.

"If you don't want to, you needn't." Revere's calm voice reassured her.

Kate's eyes met Colin's. He nodded, as though he were answering a question she had asked without speaking, and she tried to ignore the painful way her heart was thumping. Maybe it was time for her to make up her mind for herself, once and for all, the way Father had said.

"All right," she whispered. "I'll be a Patriot spy."

Harry moved closer. "You'll need to keep your wits about you all the time. Never breathe a word about what you're asked to do to anyone but Paul and me."

"Harry is right," Mr. Revere said. "With General Gage and his army getting so jumpy, there's no telling what might happen if you're caught."

"We'll be careful."

Kate swallowed the lump that suddenly formed in her throat, but she still couldn't find her voice. She let Colin speak for her.

"Tell us what you want us to do."

"Nothing right away, but be prepared. I've plans for you. Until then, keep your ears open around the redcoats. Pass along anything you see or hear to Harry."

"Yes, sir."

Kate felt like she'd just stepped off a cliff and could never again get back to safety.

CHAPTER 7
The Warning

Colin and Kate waited, frightened and excited, for their first orders as spies. A month passed, and they still hadn't been asked to do anything scary for the Patriots. They hadn't heard the redcoats whisper any secrets, either.

Sitting in her aunt and uncle's parlor, she glanced across the room at Colin. They had always been close, but now their secret was pulling them closer than ever.

The room was filled with family tonight. Kate's family and Harry's family were here. Shadows danced and darted over the families while they worked.

Colin and Harry sat close to the fireplace. They needed the light to repair the wool carders, pulling out broken wires and putting new ones in their place.

The soft whir of the great wheel as Colin's mother spun the balls into yarn was a pleasant background to the family talk.

The family used to buy much of its yarn and material, but the harbor's closing had changed all that. Most Patriots had agreed to make their own yarn and material, called homespun, instead of buying it from Britain.

Kate and Colin's sister, Isabel, were carding wool into soft balls. The wool cards were wooden paddles with hundreds of short wire teeth.

The wool was placed between two cards and combed to remove dirt and tangles. The cards' teeth made a scratching sound, like Liberty's claws when he pawed at a door to get out.

"It's so nice to spend an evening with family instead of strangers!" Kate said, pulling a fluff of wool from between her cards.

"I think it was wonderful of you to take that family into your home," Eliza said, looking up from her mending.

"Yes," Susanna agreed. She was making a pair of breeches for Colin, which he badly needed. "But it must be difficult having strangers living with you."

"It certainly is!" Kate said.

"Remember, Kate, it could have been our family chased from our home," her mother reminded her. Mama sat at the small clock wheel, winding the yarn from the great wheel onto small wooden reels.

No one said anything for a minute. Everyone knew Mama meant if the Patriots were chasing Loyalists from their homes in other towns, it could happen in Boston, too. And everyone in the room except Mama was a Patriot.

"The Patriots are wrong to chase people from their homes," Colin's mother said quietly. "We can all agree on that."

Everyone nodded.

Raised voices came from the hallway.

"It sounds like our fathers are arguing again," Kate said. She sighed and her eyes met Colin's. She saw the same pain and fright in his eyes that she felt when their fathers fought. She wasn't sure why it frightened her, but it did.

She took a deep breath. It had been such a pleasant evening, with everyone working together and visiting. Now the day would end unhappily.

Uncle Jack and her father entered the parlor, still arguing. They stopped nose-to-nose and toe-to-toe. Dr. Milton waved a copy of the *Boston Observer* in one hand. "How can you print such things?"

Uncle Jack crossed his arms. "We only printed what the Continental Congress in Philadelphia said."

Dr. Milton's eyes sparked. "You printed that Americans should not buy anything from Britain until Parliament gives up the tea tax, reopens Boston Harbor, and lets Massachusetts be run by its old charter."

"It's a peaceful way to try to get Parliament to change its mind," Uncle Jack observed. "What's wrong with that?"

Dr. Milton shook the paper right in his brother-in-law's face. "It's what you printed next that's wrong! The congress said if the redcoats attack people here, the other colonies will send troops to help Boston."

Uncle Jack grabbed the paper, crumpling it with one hand. "You think that is wrong?"

"They've almost declared war on Britain, on our own government!" Dr. Milton pushed his wig back from his forehead.

Kate choked back a giggle when she saw how funny Father looked with his wig sliding off the back of his head, but at the same time she was feeling sick to her stomach at the word "war." Everyone seemed to be using that word these days.

"John Hancock is the leader of the congress," Colin's father said. "He says we should ask God to forgive the sins that have caused our trouble with Old England. And to ask God's help in becoming friendly with England again."

Kate took a deep breath. "That sounds like the Patriots want peace, not war, Father."

Dr. Milton snorted. "Don't be fooled, Kate. The congress also said it's a Christian's duty to fight bad leaders. But the Bible says we are to obey our leaders."

"The Bible also says that rulers must be just and rule in the fear of God," Uncle Jack argued. "God wants kings to treat people well so they can live in peace and have good lives."

Harry stepped into the argument now. "Until King George rules the way the Bible says he should, we will serve no king but King Jesus."

That's the Patriots' slogan, Kate remembered. The words always sent a shiver of awe and pride through her. It seemed a great thing to choose to serve Jesus. But she knew the words only angered Loyalists like Father and Mama. After all, they served Jesus, too. They just disagreed on the way to go about doing that.

Father's fists bunched at his sides. "The congress called the king a tyrant."

Uncle Jack's face grew red. "When a king uses his power to hurt people instead of help them, he is a tyrant."

"Bah!" Dr. Milton waved both hands at him. "You make your living with words. You can make anything sound true. It's treason to declare war against the king. Treason! Until you admit as much, we're no longer friends!"

"That's fine with me!" Uncle Jack roared.

Father grabbed Kate's hand. "Come, Kate, Rosemary. We're leaving."

Kate tried to keep up with her father as she stared back over her shoulder, her wide eyes meeting Colin's. She tripped over her skirt and petticoat, and her stomach jolted. Colin's stomach clenched. What she and Colin had feared had happened—their fathers' arguments had broken their friendship.

Before the Miltons could reach the door, a loud pounding sounded outside, as though someone was insisting on entering. Kate saw that Colin had grabbed the candlestick, and now he pushed past them to answer the knocking. When he opened the door, the breeze blew the flame sideways.

Kate peered past her cousin's shoulder. There was no one on the door stoop. Only a house away, though, she saw two redcoats walking swiftly. One looked back over his shoulder with a wicked grin. Lieutenant Rand!

Why had he pounded on the door if he didn't want to come inside? A flutter caught Kate's eye. A handbill nailed to the door! Colin yanked it off and turned around.

"Who was it?" his uncle asked.

Colin didn't say anything. His face was very white. Kate looked down at the paper in his hands and saw a skull and crossbones. It made her skin crawl. She looked up at her father. "What does it mean?" she whispered.

Father's face was grim, but he didn't answer. He hesitated in the doorway, as though uncertain whether they should go or stay. Uncle Jack and Harry had come into the hallway from the parlor, and now they pressed closer to see the paper Colin held in his hand. Colin set the candlestick on a small, round piecrust table beside the door. Kate suspected he didn't want anyone to notice how badly his hands were shaking.

Colin read the paper aloud. When he got to the end, his voice was shaking as badly as his hands. " 'If fighting breaks out between the Patriots and the British troops, the Patriots' leaders will be destroyed,' " he finished.

Uncle Jack grunted. "Destroyed is a nice way to say they'll be tried in England and hung as traitors."

"Unfortunately, they are traitors." Kate thought Father's voice sounded more sad than angry now.

The paper listed Sam Adams, John Hancock, and a few others.

"Is that all it says?" Harry leaned over his younger brother's shoulder.

Colin shook his head. "There's a little bit more. 'Those trumpeters of evil, the printers, will not be forgotten.'" Kate leaned over his arm and saw that a list of Patriot printers followed. Uncle Jack's and Harry's names were at the top of the list.

CHAPTER 8
A Secret Code

Destroyed! Hung! Threats against her own uncle and cousin! Fear swept through Kate like a wildfire. The skull and crossbones seemed to laugh at them in the candlelight.

Uncle Jack picked up the paper, holding it so the candle's light fell on it. "So, Harrison, it's come." His voice was heavy.

"Yes."

Kate stared at them. How could they sound so calm? Hadn't they heard what the paper said? "Father," Colin said, his voice cracking in the way Kate knew he hated, "they've threatened your life and Harrison's."

His father, still bent over the paper, glanced at him from beneath thick black-and-gray eyebrows. "Before we can be hung, we must be brought to trial and found guilty of treason against Britain and the king. We have only printed what the congress and others said. We haven't said we agreed with them."

"That's why you've been so careful," Colin said slowly. "Sarah said you were a coward, that after General Gage brought so many troops, you didn't dare say what you thought."

"I hope we haven't been cowards. I like to think we've been wise. I've always believed that if we printed the truth, people would be smart enough to decide for themselves whether the king and

Parliament were right or whether the Patriots were right. A few years back, you'll remember I hadn't decided what I felt was the right course of action." Uncle Jack glanced at his brother-in-law, who still lingered by the doorway. "The Loyalists have several reasonable arguments, and I wanted to be sure I was not making a commitment out of emotion." He shot his oldest son a rueful smile. "Your older brother was quite impatient with me, if I remember correctly."

Harry grinned sheepishly.

"As England repeatedly infringed on our rights," Uncle Jack continued, "I came to believe in the Patriot cause. But I still was careful to print all sides of an issue in the paper. If we printed our own opinions, Harry and I could be found guilty of treason. It might come to that yet, but I hope not."

The air coming through the doorway was cold, but Kate felt suddenly damp with sweat all over. "Will you be arrested?" she asked in a small, scared voice.

Her uncle smiled at her. "We can only wait and see."

Harrison patted her shoulder. "I'm sure whoever wrote this is only trying to frighten us."

Uncle Jack nodded. "General Gage has tried to buy us—to pay us—to print only things the British government liked. Lieutenant Rand threatened us the other day. Now this."

Colin stood up a little straighter. "I think Lieutenant Rand nailed this to our door. I saw him on the street."

His father sighed. "It would be like him to use his position to try to bully us. Thank God all the British officers aren't like him." He folded the paper in half and turned to look at his wife through the parlor's open doorway. Kate saw that her aunt and the other women were sitting frozen, their faces very white. "Don't fret over this," Uncle Jack said, his voice strong and calm. "We are in the Lord's hands."

Kate watched as Harry went back into the parlor and took down the old musket that hung over the fireplace. He ran a hand along the barrel. The musket had been there for as long as Kate could remember.

"Do you think it works?" Colin asked.

"I don't know. I'm not sure we can get ammunition for it. It's awfully old. Our great-grandfather, Robert, carried it to war against the French in 1710. He fought alongside the British soldiers then. Now if we fight with it, we'll be fighting against the British."

Kate saw Colin's Adam's apple jerk, as though he were fighting back a lump in his throat. "He was killed in that war. Our grand-father, his only child, was born while he was fighting, remember? He never even saw his son."

Harrison nodded, his eyes grave.

Colin stuck his hands in his breeches' deep pockets. "Do you think that might happen to your son, Paul, if you fight? If you were. . .if you were killed—"

Kate gulped and fought back the tears that burned her eyes.

"You'd never see Paul again," Colin finished, his voice cracking. "He's only six months old. He might not even remember you when he grows up."

"I know." Harry's words were so low that Kate almost didn't hear them. Harry carefully hung the musket back in place. "I've joined the minutemen." He turned and looked at his wife. "I have to do what I believe is right."

"I thought you would." Colin's voice was barely more than a whisper.

"I talked it over with Eliza first," Harry said. "I do think about Paul. I worry what will happen to him and Eliza if we go to war. But

Eliza and I agreed that when Paul grows up, we want him to have the rights Englishmen have had for more than five hundred years—even if that means I have to fight."

Kate's father moved as if to go out the door. She knew he didn't want to hear any of this, that he did not want to be associated with what he considered treason. But she could tell by the look on his face that he also hated to leave. After all, Colin's mother was his sister. They were family. No matter how much Father and Uncle Jack argued, Kate knew her father loved his family.

"What about you?" Harry asked Colin.

Colin frowned. "What do you mean?"

"If war comes, will you fight with the Patriots?"

Colin shrugged and kicked at a bit of ash on the floor with the toe of his shoe. "I won't fight against them."

Harry grinned. "I didn't think you would, but that's no answer. You're thirteen, almost a man."

Colin squared his shoulders. "I don't know if I can try to kill anyone. I want to be a doctor and save lives." He turned and looked at his uncle, then looked back at his brother. "Have you ever seen anyone die?"

Harrison shook his head. "No."

"I have, lots of times. It's terrible. Uncle Firth and I do everything we can sometimes—and yet people still die." He pressed his lips together hard and spread his hands. "Do you understand? Life is precious. When I know how hard it is to save a life, how can I choose to kill? It's much easier to take a life than save one."

Kate knew her father was proud of his nephew's words. But would Harrison understand? She held her breath, waiting for Harry's reply. Colin put so much stock in his brother's good opinion. He would be crushed if this war came between him and his brother.

Harrison sighed. "You have a good head on your shoulders, Colin. You don't let anyone push you into anything you don't believe in. That's good." He, too, glanced at his uncle. "I've heard Uncle Firth say more than once that each man has to make up his mind for himself. I respect that. But what if everyone refused to fight and let King George take away all our rights? What would our children and grandchildren say when they found out we'd let our rights be taken away without a fight? If war comes, you may not have a choice but to fight. The only choice left will be which side you fight for."

Kate's gaze slid to the musket, almost hidden now in the room's dark shadows. The dull gray metal on the musket's barrel looked cold in the firelight—and a chill that was just as icy wrapped itself tight around her heart.

"Come along, Kate," her mother whispered. "It's time for us to go."

The next morning, Kate looked out the apothecary window and saw Colin standing outside beneath the creaking sign with the mortar and pestle. His hands were bunched into fists at his sides.

Kate pulled a cloak around her shoulders and ran out into the street. "What are you doing?"

He shrugged, his face worried. "Does your father still want me to be his apprentice? After what happened yesterday. . .will he even want you and I to be friends?"

"Well, you won't find out standing in the street," Kate replied. "Come inside and find out."

Colin took a deep breath and went inside.

Kate's father looked up from his account book. "Colin, I'm glad you're here! I was afraid your father might not let you come after last night."

Kate heard Colin let out a long breath of relief. "He didn't tell me I couldn't come, but I was afraid you might not want me."

Dr. Milton laid down his quill. His gaze met Colin's. "My argument is with your father, not with you. I count you not only my apprentice and nephew, but my friend."

"Thank you, sir, but I–I'm a Patriot, too, like Father."

"Do you think King George is a tyrant?"

"I'm not sure. When I hear you talk about what you believe about the king and our rights, what you say sounds right. But I think what Father believes is more right, and I believe what Father believes."

"At least you listen to both sides. You aren't encouraging anyone to fight like your father is."

"No, sir." Colin frowned, and Kate knew he was uneasy with her father's words. What would Father say if he knew she had promised to help spy for the Patriots?

"Your father is a stubborn man." Her father grinned. "But your aunt Rosemary says I'm one, too. Don't worry yourself over your father and me. We've been angry at each other before. We'll work things out eventually. Now, let's get to work, you two. There are some plants in the medical garden that need to be picked and dried."

In spite of her father's assurances, Kate wasn't convinced the men would work things out. The two had quarreled a lot through the years, but Kate had never seen them as angry at each other as they were now. At least Father still wanted Colin to be his apprentice. She was glad this one thing in life was the same. She couldn't imagine life without Colin.

At eleven o'clock, Kate ran home and brought back lunch for her father and Larry.

"I know you brought your own lunch," she said to Colin, "but I brought you a piece of apple pie."

"Great!"

She wrinkled her nose. "Not too great. It's Boston Tea Party apple pie. We're out of sugar and good flour, so I sweetened it with honey, and the crust is of cornmeal." All the women in town were using substitutes in their cooking. With the port closed, many of the foods they were used to using couldn't be found in Boston or were too expensive to buy.

"Mother and I try to make a game of it, figuring out how to make our favorite dishes using different foods. Some things turn out better than others." Kate sighed.

Two days later, when Kate stopped at Colin's house, she noticed the musket was gone from over the fireplace. She didn't ask where it went. Patriots were collecting weapons in case of war. But the thought of Harry with a gun in his hand made her shiver.

But something else pushed all thought of the musket from her mind. She and Colin were given a spy assignment!

Kate's father had asked Colin to take Larry home to his farm near Lexington, and Kate was going to ride along. When Harry and Paul Revere heard, they told Colin to take some copies of the *Boston Observer* to Buckman's Tavern in Lexington.

"There's a hidden message in the newspaper," Harrison had said, stacking the single sheets into a pile.

Colin laughed. "You can't hide anything in a newspaper!"

"The best place to hide anything is right in plain sight." Harry's eyes twinkled with fun. "The message becomes clear when the reader uses a mask to read it."

"You're funning us," Kate giggled. "How can wearing a mask help?"

"Maybe the mask has spectacles with magic glass," Colin teased.

"It's not that kind of mask. The reader doesn't wear the mask. He lays the mask over the newspaper. Like this." Harry showed Kate and Colin a cutout of the picture that was always printed at the top of the *Boston Observer*. It was a man looking through a telescope. The inside of the picture had been cut out. Harry laid the mask over the covered page. "See for yourself."

Colin grinned. "You're just waiting for me to make a fool of myself and try to find a secret message where there is none. Like the time I was six and you told me there were fish in Mill Pond that could walk. I fished and watched for those walking fish for weeks before Susanna told me you were only teasing!"

Harry crossed his arms over his vest and chuckled. "This is no walking fish, I promise. Look."

Kate and Colin looked. The mask was small. The opening only covered ten lines of the tiny type, and two of the six narrow columns. The message inside the cutout included words from more than one column. Kate's mouth dropped open as she read them. "Why, this says—"

Harry clapped a hand that smelled strongly of ink and leather over Kate's mouth. "Never repeat a message aloud, even when you think you're alone or with someone you can trust, like now. You only need to be wrong one time to get in a lot of trouble."

Kate and Colin both nodded, their smiles fading.

Harry took away his hand. "Now that redcoats are checking everyone who comes into and leaves Boston, the Patriots are trying new ways to get messages to each other safely. Sometimes the messages will be true. Sometimes they will be false, used only to test whether people can be trusted or are spies for the British. You're never to tell anyone you're carrying a message or what it says."

"We won't," Colin promised.

Harry glanced at Kate, and she nodded. "I give my word." It was hard to speak past the lump in her throat.

Harry grinned. "Your word is always good enough for me."

Colin was studying the mask. "How does the person who gets the message know what part of the paper to put the mask over so he reads the right words?"

"That's a secret you'll never know."

CHAPTER 9

Escape from Boston

A few days later, Larry, Colin, Kate, and Liberty sat together in Dr. Milton's carriage. Every once in a while, Larry's leg bounced against the side when a wooden wheel rolled over a rock or rut. Larry would grunt and dig his teeth into his bottom lip, but he never complained. Kate admired him for that. She knew Larry's leg was still mighty sore and would be for weeks.

"Whoa." Colin pulled on the reins, bringing Dr. Milton's small bay mare to a stop at the town gate on the Neck. Redcoats were checking everyone who left town now. In front of them, a farmer with an empty cart waited patiently behind another farmer with an empty wagon.

One of the redcoats knelt down and looked beneath the wagon, then stood and felt beneath the hard wooden seat the farmer sat upon. A moment later he waved the farmer on.

"They're lookin' for guns," Larry said in a low voice. "They've heard Patriots are sneakin' guns out of Boston."

Goose bumps ran up and down Kate's arms. Had Harry slipped the musket past the guards somehow?

Woof! Liberty's bark startled Kate. In a flash, the skinny dog scrambled across her lap and leaped from the carriage after a squirrel.

"Liberty, stop!"

Liberty ignored his mistress's cry. The squirrel darted under the farmer's moving wagon, and Liberty headed after him.

Kate leaped to her feet. Liberty was going to be run over! "Stop, Liberty!"

A farmer with a cart in front of them dove for Liberty. He caught his skinny tail and held tight. Liberty yelped a complaint, but the farmer yanked him back, saving him from the wagon's rumbling wheels. He handed Liberty up to Kate with a friendly grin.

"Thank you, sir. Guess you saved his life."

"A life worth saving, I'm sure. Have a dog of me own I wouldn't trade for King George's palace."

The soldiers were searching the farmer's cart. It didn't take long. When they waved the farmer on, he gave them a jaunty salute before starting.

"Halt!" One of the soldiers pointed his musket at the farmer. "I know you! Deserter!"

Kate's heart seemed to leap to her throat. She watched, stunned, as the soldiers arrested the man who had cheerfully saved Liberty's life.

Kate and Colin looked at each other. A deserter! Larry shrugged nervously. "We've nothin' to worry 'bout. We're not sneakin' anyone or anything out of town."

Kate's foot touched the pile of newspapers on the floor. Larry didn't know they carried a Patriot secret.

The redcoat who had checked the cart waved for Colin to move forward, and Colin clicked his tongue at the horse. The soldier looked underneath the carriage. Then he ordered Kate, Colin, and Larry to get out.

Kate forced herself to not look at the newspapers as she climbed down.

"Larry has a bad leg," Colin told the soldier. "He hurt it working on the wall here on the Neck. Can he stay in the carriage? It still hurts him a lot to walk on it."

The soldier looked into the carriage and reached for Larry's leg. His hand stopped above the bandages. Larry had no stocking on that leg. It was still too swollen and too heavily wrapped for a stocking to fit. "Stay where you are, then," he told Larry.

The soldier pointed to the pile. "Are those rebel Patriot newspapers or Loyalist newspapers?"

"Just newspapers, sir."

Pretend everything is normal, Kate commanded him silently.

"The editor prints facts, not opinions."

The redcoat grunted. "I'll be deciding that for myself. Let me see one of them rags."

Larry untied the twine that held the papers together and handed him one off the top. The soldier glanced over it. "Why, this tells all about that rebel Patriot congress in Philadelphia!" His eyes looked like small black beads as he glared over the top of the page at Colin. "Says the colonies should train their armies in case we attack them! What do you mean saying this isn't a rebel paper?"

"Only tells what the congress said, sir. Doesn't tell the readers to do as the congress asks. Besides, there's a Loyalist handbill we're carrying as well."

Colin pulled out a handbill topped by a skull and crossbones and handed it to the soldier. It was the same handbill that threatened his father's and Harry's lives. "You see, the editor prints news for both Patriots and Loyalists."

"You the printer's apprentice?" The soldier raised one black eyebrow and eyed Colin suspiciously.

"Oh, no, sir! I'm Dr. Milton's apprentice. This is his carriage. I'm taking his patient home to his farm."

The soldier grunted again. "Dr. Milton's a good Loyalist."

"Yes, sir. Can't find a man more loyal to the king."

"Sure wish I hadn't hurt this leg." Larry rubbed his knee and shook his head. "Wanted to keep helpin' build that wall for General Gage. Lot more excitin' than farmin'."

The redcoat handed Larry back the paper and handbill. "Have any good fishing streams on that farm?"

"The best in Massachusetts, sir. I plan to take the children here fishin' there today."

"Maybe you'll bring a few fish back for me?" The soldier grinned, showing three of his teeth were missing on one side of his mouth.

"Be glad to, sir." Colin climbed back into the carriage.

He and Kate waved and smiled at the soldier as they drove off. When they'd gone about one hundred feet, Colin let his breath out in a whoosh. "I didn't think he was going to let us take those papers with us."

"Me, either. Redcoats have good guns and cannons, but it's words that scare them."

They both laughed at that.

Kate hadn't been out of Boston in months. She felt suddenly free out on the road.

Once they reached Lexington, it was easy to find Buckman's Tavern, a two-story wooden building with two chimneys. It stood by the town common, called Lexington Green. The road ran right past the green.

The tavern master gave no hint that he knew the papers held a secret message. Kate wondered if he was the man who knew how to read the message. Or maybe it was one of the tavern workers or a stable boy who watched the guests' horses. Could it be the craftsman who walked in and bought a copy almost right away?

A spy could be anyone, Kate realized. She giggled. Who, for instance, would think she was a spy?

"What's so funny?" Larry asked her.

"Just glad to be out of Boston for a change." She exchanged glances with Colin, and they both grinned.

The tavern keeper gave them each a mug of cold apple cider. They took their drinks outside and sat on the edge of the green beneath a large oak tree. The ground was covered with brown, musty-smelling leaves that crackled beneath Kate's skirts when she sat down. The dampness from the earth seeped through the leaves and through her petticoat and skirt, but she hardly noticed.

The Lexington minutemen were practicing on the green. Back home, the minutemen couldn't practice on Boston Common, what with the redcoats living and training there.

Watching the men, Kate's good spirits suddenly deserted her, and her heart sank as fast as a rock to the bottom of one of Boston's ponds. Lexington's army looked like a ragtag group of boys playing at war compared to the redcoats. The minutemen were dressed in their everyday work clothes: craftsmen in leather breeches and rough shirts, farmers in frocks, storekeepers and town leaders in fancy greatcoats and long vests. No one wore a uniform. Not one carried a musket as fine as the redcoats' muskets. Instead they held squirrel and duck rifles or old muskets like the one that had hung over the Lang fireplace. A few men who'd fought in the French and Indian Wars years ago had swords at their sides. No one had a bayonet like the redcoats had on the ends of their muskets.

The minutemen didn't snap to orders with sharp attention like the redcoats on Boston Common. They didn't move as one person to the officers' orders. Kate wondered whether they even knew how poorly they compared to the redcoats. The men tramping through the crisp leaves beneath the bright blue sky were eagerly trying to follow commands, their eyes shining, their faces excited.

"Why don't they practice shooting?" Colin asked Larry.

"Savin' their bullets. With General Gage and his men raidin' towns' ammunition, we don't dare waste any."

The longer Colin and Larry watched, the sadder Kate grew. Harry was part of Boston's minutemen. Were they as poorly furnished and trained as these men? If a war started, what chance did Harry and the minutemen have against the redcoats?

"I'm goin' to join the minutemen," Larry said, "soon's my leg's better."

"Do you have a gun?" Colin asked.

"Only an old squirrel gun, but I can shoot with it." Larry leaned back against the tree. "Shot lots of squirrels and rabbits and such. A man should be easy to hit."

Kate's stomach turned over at the thought of shooting a man like he was wild game.

When the practice was over, a boy carrying a large drum and a handful of men with fifes started playing "Yankee Doodle" and started across the green. The minutemen fell in behind them. They headed toward a large wooden building beside Buckman's Tavern.

Colin jumped up. "Where are they going?"

"To the meeting house," Larry said. "A Patriot minister will give them a sermon tellin' them to fight bravely for God and their country." He got slowly to his feet. "I'd like to be getting home, if you don't mind."

Larry kept his word and took the cousins fishing at a stream that ran through his father's property. It was the most fun Kate had had in a long time. When she and Colin headed back to Boston later that afternoon, a huge basket with sixty smelly perch sat between them on the floor of the carriage. Larry's father and mother had also sent back pumpkins, corn, and flour for the doctor. "There's barely room left for me," Kate had told Larry with a grin.

Colin didn't forget the soldier at the gate. When they arrived there late that evening, he gave him a dozen fish. The soldier grinned from ear to ear as he piled the fish on the ground beside the gate, where they would lie until the soldier was off duty.

"Remember that deserter we caught this afternoon?" the soldier asked, taking the last fish Colin handed him.

Kate's heart thumped so hard she could barely hear herself think. Why would the redcoat ask Colin about the deserter? Had he somehow learned Colin had slipped a secret message out of town right beneath his nose?

Beside her, Colin gulped and wiped his hand on his breeches. "Sure, I remember. He was dressed like a farmer."

"They shot him this afternoon on the common." The soldier grinned. "General Gage came out personally to tell me and the other guard here how well we'd done in capturing him."

"Congratulations," Colin said in a shaky voice. "Good night, sir. Enjoy your fish." He reached for the reins and slapped them lightly against the horse's rump.

Kate's eyes were too blurry with tears for her to see the road ahead. Other redcoat deserters had been shot, but she hadn't known who they were. She hadn't seen them captured only a few feet from freedom. They hadn't smiled at her and saved her dog.

Suddenly, Kate pulled desperately on Colin's arm. She was going to be sick.

CHAPTER 10

A Dangerous Mission

Six weeks later, Kate gritted her teeth as she came through the door of Colin's house. The first thing she heard was a voice she'd grown to dislike: Lieutenant Rand's. She wondered for the hundredth time how Lieutenant Rand had been assigned to live in her uncle's house!

Winter was coming, and many British officers were staying in townspeople's houses. Quartering, it was called. But why Lieutenant Rand of all people?

Kate stepped softly past the parlor, where the officers were visiting, toward the kitchen. She caught a glimpse of the firelight and candlelight that gave the parlor a mellow glow, but the hallway was dark and shadowed. Until the officers had moved in, the family had saved scarce wood and candles by keeping the parlor closed. They visited by the kitchen fireplace instead. There the wood could be used for three things at once: It heated the room, heated food, and heated water for washing and chores. Now, though, they were forced to waste expensive fuel and light on the redcoats.

"You there, lass!" Lieutenant Rand's voice stopped her before she could reach the kitchen.

Kate sighed and walked into the warm parlor. "Yes, sir?"

"See that someone polishes my boots."

Kate's cheeks grew hot. She pressed her lips hard together to keep from telling the officer to polish his own boots. Her uncle had warned them all to treat the officers like guests. "Yes, Lieutenant Rand," she managed to say meekly. "I'll tell my cousin."

"See he does a better job than he did last week."

"Yes, sir." Kate looked at the other officer, who stood before the fireplace with his elbow on the mantel, frowning at Lieutenant Rand. "Shall I have Colin polish your boots, too, Lieutenant Andrews?"

The senior officer smiled at her. "No, but it was kind of you to offer."

Kate nodded at both men and made her way back to the kitchen. At least Lieutenant Andrews acted kindly toward the family. Still, she liked having the officers in Colin's home even less than she liked having them in her own. What if they found reason to arrest Uncle Jack or Harry?

She knew the officers had taken over the bedchamber Harrison shared with his wife, Eliza, and their son, Paul. Now Harrison's family used Colin's bedchamber, and Colin slept on the high-backed wooden settle beside the kitchen fireplace.

He tried not to complain about it. Officers were quartered all over town. Uncle Thomas had officers staying with him, and so did Kate's family. But Kate knew how much it galled Colin to have to give up his room because of the redcoats.

As Kate slipped into the warm kitchen, her aunt greeted her with a warm smile. "Ah, Kate, it's always good to see you." Kate knew the disagreement between her father and uncle pained her aunt. "Colin was just saying he was hoping you'd come by."

Kate glanced at her cousin where he sat whittling by the fire. "Want to take a stroll with me?" he asked, setting aside the knife.

She nodded, wondering why Colin felt a sudden urge to walk

around the chilly streets. But as soon as they were outside the kitchen door, Harry stepped out of a doorway across the street, as though he'd been standing there waiting for them.

"Are you staying for supper, Kate?" Harry asked in a low voice.

She nodded, wondering why he looked so serious.

"I need to talk with you two." Harry glanced at the house. "Make an excuse after the meal to slip out to the print shop."

Kate looked at the empty street and frowned. "Why not talk here?"

"Walls have ears these days. And windows have eyes."

Colin nodded. And Kate realized that with the officers here, it wasn't safe for them to talk about Patriot matters even in the street. She wondered what could be so important that they had to go somewhere tonight to talk. Could the Sons of Liberty have another spying assignment for them?

A little later when she joined her aunt and uncle and cousins for the evening meal, she noticed that Susanna and Lieutenant Andrews were in the doorway between the parlor and hallway. Kate wondered why Susanna was smiling up at the British officer in that funny, sugary-sweet way with her cheeks all pink. Could Susanna like Lieutenant Andrews? Not just friendly-like, but as a woman likes a man? Could Susanna be falling in love with someone who wasn't a Patriot?

When they finished dinner, Lieutenant Rand pushed back his chair. "I'll have a cup of tea in the parlor, Miss Susanna. See that it's good English tea—none of your rebel Patriot brew."

Everyone stopped talking and stared at him. Finally Susanna stood. Her long red curls reflected the light from the few candles that burned on the table. "I'll be glad to bring you tea, sir." Her voice trembled. "But I'm afraid it will be raspberry leaf tea. We don't serve

English tea in this house. English tea has brought too much trouble to our town."

Lieutenant Rand threw down his napkin. "No lady in England would treat a guest like this!"

"Lieutenant Rand!" Lieutenant Andrews sounded shocked.

Uncle Jack leaped up. "Apologize to my daughter!"

Lieutenant Rand snorted and ignored Uncle Jack's demand.

Susanna paid no attention. "Lieutenant Rand, in Boston, no gentleman asks for anything he knows his host is not able or willing to give."

Good for her! Kate thought, her hands clenched into fists beneath the table.

Red color started at Lieutenant Rand's neck and rushed up over his face to his wig. He turned to Lieutenant Andrews. "If anyone asks for me this evening, I'll be at Dr. Milton's." He glared over his shoulder at Susanna. "The Miltons know how to treat their guests." He stomped toward the door, his boots thunking against the floor.

Harry gave Kate a strange look. "I didn't know Lieutenant Rand knew your father."

Kate nodded. "Officers are quartered at my house, too. They use my father's library in the evenings instead of going to the taverns like most soldiers." She wrinkled her nose. "They expect us to wait on them, just like Lieutenant Rand."

"I apologize for our officers," Lieutenant Andrews said. "I know it's hard for people to have us living in their homes. Please remember that it's hard for the officers, too. They'd rather be in their own homes with their own families back in England."

Susanna smiled at him. "Of course they would."

Kate wondered again how Susanna felt about the kind, good-looking young officer.

A few minutes later, Kate, Colin, and Harry were headed toward the print shop, their cloaks wrapped tightly against the cold November wind whipping through Boston's narrow streets. They had to watch where they were going, as the streetlights weren't lit. The town had only had streetlights for a year and a half, and Kate had thought they were the most wonderful invention she'd ever seen. She liked watching the men climb their ladders each night with their oil cans to light the lamps. Now, though, the town couldn't even use them. People couldn't buy lamp oil when money was so tight.

Kate wondered all the way to the printing shop what Harry would tell them. The redcoats they passed in the street reminded her why they had to be so cautious. A fourth of the people in Boston now were British soldiers. Many of the other people were Loyalists. Patriots had to be careful what they said everywhere.

"Brrr! It's almost as cold inside as out!" Colin rubbed his mittened hands together after entering the shop.

Harry reached in his pocket for a flint to light a candle. The flint sparked and the candlewick flared. Its yellow flame gave a small circle of light but left most of the room with its press and piles of paper in dark shadows.

"What do you have to tell us?" Kate couldn't wait any longer.

Harry hiked himself onto the wooden worktable beside the candle. "The Observers have another assignment for you two."

Kate's heartbeat quickened, but Colin sounded calm as he said, "Do they want us to sneak more newspapers out of town?"

"No. This is far more dangerous."

"What. . .what is it?"

"A redcoat wants to desert. He needs help getting out of Boston."

Kate shivered. She remembered the deserter arrested at the Neck.

"Deserters are killed if they're caught." Her voice trembled.

"Yes."

"What happens to people who help them?" Colin asked, and his voice sounded shaky, too.

"Prison. Still want to help us?"

Kate took a deep breath. This was scarier than she'd thought it would be.

"Yes," Colin said. "But I don't see how we can get anyone past the guards on the Neck in Uncle Firth's carriage."

"You won't need to. You just need to hide him for one night, give him different clothes to wear, and hide his uniform."

"Where can we hide him?" Kate asked. "Officers are living with both of us! Do you mean to hide him here in the print shop?"

"No. The redcoats are watching this place too closely. We want you to hide him at the apothecary shop for a few hours."

Kate frowned. "The apothecary is full of officers and Loyalists. How could we hide him there? Father would never let us."

Harry smiled. "It's like the hidden message in the newspaper. The best place to hide something or someone is in plain sight. No one will think it strange to see a soldier go into a Loyalist doctor's place. Your father need never know. Now, here's the plan."

CHAPTER 11
The Deserter

Kate was so excited she didn't fall asleep until very late. She tossed and turned, trying to think where she could hide the deserter in the apothecary shop. How could she keep Father from finding out?

When she finally did fall asleep, she dreamed she and Colin were standing in front of a redcoats' firing squad! She woke up sweating.

The next morning, Colin met her outside the apothecary shop with a burlap sack under his arm. "Is that your lunch?" she asked him, though she was pretty sure it wasn't. She clutched her ankle-length cape over her warm quilted skirt to keep away the November chill.

"That's right," he said. "I have an enormous hunger today. Comes from all those stingy meals we've been having. Want to see what I've got?"

He held the top of the sack open so she could see the folded petticoats and woman's gown and wig. Kate knew they were for the deserter. "Mmm," she said, her eyes dancing. "It looks delicious."

All day, as Kate and Colin worked inside the apothecary, Harry's plan was all Kate could think about. They didn't know when the deserter would show up. He would have to watch closely for a chance to get away from the other redcoats without raising suspicion.

Kate watched for the deserter all day. And all the next day. By the third day, she was beginning to wonder if the soldier would ever show up. But she forgot about him for hours at a time while she worked. Putting together the different medicines fascinated her.

She tried to remember everything her father said about which plants healed what ailments. Someday, when she was grown up and all this Patriot and Loyalist business was somehow behind them, she was determined that she would be a healer. Even if she had to leave Boston and go live in some wilderness community far to the west. Maybe when she was older, she could find a midwife who would take her as a sort of apprentice.

Her daydreams made the day go faster. By the time she and Colin were closing up the shop, it was long past candle-lighting time. Before they finished, the officers quartered with the Miltons came through the shop on their way to the house. Colin carried wood and started a fire for them in the library fireplace while one of the officers lit what seemed to Kate to be a wasteful number of candles.

Kate had just gone back into the apothecary to bar the door when she heard a knock outside. She swung the door open. A redcoat with brown curly hair stood there. He wasn't an officer. "Are you looking for the officers, sir?" Kate asked him.

"No, I'm looking for a doctor. I've cut my hand."

"The doctor's visiting patients. I'm his daughter. Come in. I'll fetch my father's apprentice." She called Colin to come in from the library. Her cousin placed a tin lantern on a table and unwrapped the bloody cloth from the redcoat's hand. Colin studied the wound in the light.

"I was polishing my bayonet," the redcoat said, "and it slipped. How bad is the cut?"

"Not as bad as it looks," Colin said. "Even though it bled a lot, it will be fine when the wound heals."

The man gave a large sigh of relief. "Good." He set his hat on the table. "What are your names?"

"Colin Lang. And this is my cousin, Kate Milton." Colin started to go get clean bandages, but the soldier's good hand clamped Colin's shoulder and stopped him. Colin's head jerked up in surprise.

"God bless the Liberty Boys," the man whispered.

Kate blinked. That was the code Harry had said the deserter would use!

The door into the Milton home swung open and Captain Ingles came in. He was a large, kind man, but Kate's heart was beating so loudly in her ears that she could hardly think. Had the captain heard the code? No, he couldn't have heard them from behind the thick door! The soldier had only whispered.

Seeing the captain, the injured redcoat snapped to his feet in attention. The captain waved a pudgy hand. "Sit down. Heard the bells on the shop door ring when you came in." He studied the soldier's hand. "Nasty wound there."

"I looked for the troop's doctor. When I couldn't find him, I came here."

Colin stood up. "I can take care of it, sir."

The captain looked down his thick nose into Colin's eyes. "I shouldn't be surprised if you can. The doctor speaks highly of you, lad."

Colin grinned with pride. "Thank you, sir."

"Show the other officers to the library when they arrive, will you, miss? There's a good lass."

When the library door shut behind the captain, Colin looked at Kate. She wondered what they should do next. Should she repeat the code, so the deserter would know he'd found the right place?

But what if he wasn't the deserter? What if the redcoats had found out about the plan and this man was here to trap them? Kate raised her eyebrows at Colin, trying to ask him silently what they should do next.

Colin seemed as lost as she was. He rubbed his hands down the thighs of his homespun breeches. "Thread me a needle, Kate," he said. "I'm going to take a couple stitches so the wound will heal faster."

While Kate threaded the curved needle, her mind raced. They could play it safe. They could pretend the man's words meant nothing to them. But if he *were* the deserter and Colin and Kate didn't help him, would he ever have another chance to get away?

The man held his wounded hand in the candlelight while Colin bent his head over the wound and made his stitches. When he was done, while their heads were still close together above the tin lantern, Kate heard her cousin whisper, "God bless the Liberty Boys."

Liberty, who had been sleeping in a ball beneath the table, heard his name and sat up. He thudded his skinny tail against the floor and whined.

Kate giggled. "Not you, boy." She explained to the soldier about Liberty's name.

The soldier's face lit up in a smile. He patted Liberty's head. "Thought I'd made a mistake when you didn't repeat the code." He spoke in a whisper.

"Are you going to come back after the officers go to bed?" Colin asked.

The soldier shook his head. "I'm not leaving. When it's discovered I'm missing, the officers will remember I was here. The officer saw my wound, so they'll know I was hurt. I'm hoping they won't think you or this place have anything to do with my escape."

Colin led the soldier over to the waist-high wooden counter and opened two doors beneath the counter. Then he looked the soldier up and down. He wasn't a tall man, and he wasn't large or fat, either, but he had broad shoulders.

"I thought this would be the perfect place to hide you," Colin whispered. "Some doctors' apprentices sleep on shelves in doctors' apothecaries. But I'm not sure you'll fit."

Kate had emptied the cupboard earlier. She'd even taken out the middle shelf to make more room.

The soldier squatted down and held the lantern by the tin handle at the top so it shone into the cupboard. "A bit of a tight squeeze, perhaps, but I think I can make it." He stood, set the lantern down, and held out his good hand. "Thank you, Colin Lang." He gave Kate a little bow. "I'll never forget the chance you two are taking for me. My name is George Lambert. I hope we'll meet again someday, when the redcoats have left Boston."

George Lambert turned toward the cupboard. "Go open the door, Kate. Pretend I'm leaving, Colin."

Kate did as she was told. She glanced up and down the street to see whether there was anyone that might see. She saw only a couple lantern flickers too far away for the people carrying them to tell whether anyone stood before the apothecary. In a loud voice, Colin wished Mr. Lambert Godspeed and told him to come back in a couple days to have the doctor look at his wound.

Then Colin hurried back to the counter. He pointed to a cloth bag in the cupboard. "Your new clothes are in there."

"Daren't change now. I'd better try out my new home before the officers come out here." Lambert grinned.

Laughing voices outside the door startled them. Lambert scuttled into the cupboard, drawing his knees up beneath his chin. Colin closed the doors just as Lieutenant Rand and another officer entered.

Kate bit her bottom lip hard. If there was anyone they didn't want to see, it was Lieutenant Rand! No one would rather catch a Lang with a deserter than that man.

Lieutenant Rand was carrying a tray with pewter mugs and a tall bottle. "We were hoping to have some hot punch. Make us some, lass." He glanced at Colin as he set the tray down on the countertop. "Working late, lad?"

Colin nodded and continued to put away the various medicines he had used that day. Kate hurried to fetch from the kitchen a large silver bowl with oranges, lemons, and spices in it. She could have made the punch over the kitchen fire, but she decided to use the stove in the apothecary instead. She wanted to keep an eye on Lieutenant Rand.

As she came back into the shop, a movement across the room caught her attention. Liberty was playing with Mr. Lambert's hat! Her feet seemed to freeze to the floor. She glanced at Colin, but he seemed not to have noticed. What if Rand saw that hat? He mustn't!

Liberty and the hat were in the shadows. Rand might not recognize the hat if he didn't get close to it. But what if Liberty dragged it closer? The best thing to do would be to go right over and pick up the hat, like nothing was wrong, she decided.

She almost had to pick up her feet with her hands to make them move, she was so scared. As she walked, she untied her white apron. When she reached Liberty, the dog thumped his tail, thinking Kate was going to play. Kate dropped her apron on top of the hat, then stooped and picked up both hat and apron together. Liberty caught one of the apron's ties in his teeth and growled playfully. "No! Down!" Kate ordered.

Liberty tucked his head.

"You hurt his feelings," Colin said as he put the last bottle away. "He just wants to play."

"Stupid mutt." Lieutenant Rand started toward the library. Liberty darted under a chair. The dog had learned that Lieutenant Rand's boots had a way of kicking him if he wasn't careful.

As Lieutenant Rand passed him, Kate bundled the apron closer around the hat. "Always cloths and aprons to wash out when you work in a doctor's apothecary," she complained.

Lieutenant Rand made a face and quickly left the room.

Kate breathed a sigh of relief. She'd never have gotten away with it if it had been daylight! At the counter, she opened the door, threw in the hat and apron, and slammed the door shut.

Colin looked at her as though she had lost her mind. "Lambert's hat," Kate said under her breath as she leaned close to her cousin. "It was on the floor."

Colin turned pale as he realized the close call they had had. Silently, they worked together making the punch. Kate's mouth watered at the wonderful smells of the oranges and lemons when she sliced them.

"Well, that's one advantage of having the officers quartered with us," Kate said. "They can get the best food. We can't afford fruit like this anymore."

Colin didn't look as though he had heard her. "What are we going to do?" he whispered. "How are we going to get Lambert on his way without the officers seeing?"

Kate frowned. Then she remembered something she had just learned. She smiled. "I have an idea."

CHAPTER 12

A Safely Delivered "Package"

Captain Ingles came into the shop. "Bring us more firewood, lad. We plan to be here a while."

Colin hurried to get the wood, while Kate watched him with her heart in her mouth. Every minute the soldiers spent in the library was another minute of danger for the deserting soldier—and for her and Colin! Would her idea work?

She scraped the hard brown nutmeg against the tin grater, then handed it to Colin when he came from the library. While he sprinkled the spice into the punch, she ground some of her father's herbs in a mortar.

"What's that?" Colin asked as she poured the crushed herbs into the punch.

Kate smiled. "Just something new." She held up the herbs so he could see what she was using.

Colin's eyes widened. "What if it makes the punch taste funny?"

Kate shook her head. "The officers will like it fine." She knew the taste of the fruit and spices would be stronger than the herb's. And the herb made people sleepy. They would have to use a lot of it in the punch to be sure it had the effect she wanted. She only hoped it would work and send the men to their beds early.

Kate and Colin carried the bowl and mugs into the library. Kate used a dipper to fill the mugs. Captain Ingles smacked his lips and reached for a poker heating in the fireplace. The poker sizzled when he stuck it in his mug to warm the spiced punch.

Lieutenant Rand picked up a mug. "At least there's one family in Boston that knows how to give an Englishman good food."

Kate clenched her teeth and shot a warning glance at Colin. She knew Lieutenant Rand was reminding them that Susanna wouldn't serve him English tea.

Kate started rearranging books on a shelf near the library door. It was a good place to stand to try to overhear the officers, so she often pretended to be busy there.

Woof! Woof!

Kate whirled around at Liberty's yelp. Liberty was usually too well behaved to bark inside!

Liberty was in front of the cupboard door. His nose was almost on the floor. His rear end, with its tail going a mile a minute, was stuck up in the air.

Something red on the floor in front of Liberty moved. A piece of Mr. Lambert's uniform! Lambert was trying to pull it back inside without opening the door. Liberty jumped on the moving cloth with another yelp. He growled playfully, tugging the cloth back and forth.

"What's all the noise?" Lieutenant Rand bellowed from the doorway. Kate's heart leaped right into her throat at his unexpected voice.

"I'm sorry, sir. My dog must have seen a mouse!" Kate said loudly.

"Can't you keep that mutt quiet?"

"We're trying, sir," Colin said. He knelt beside Liberty, hiding the piece of red cloth. If Lieutenant Rand saw the cloth, he'd be sure to know it was part of a redcoat's uniform!

"Dogs don't belong inside anyway," Rand muttered, closing the library door.

It wasn't easy to make Liberty let go of the cloth, but Colin finally did. "We'd better put Liberty outside."

Kate scrunched up her face. "But it's cold out! And what if those rough boys find him again?"

Colin glared at her. "He's endangering a man's life!" He scooped Liberty up in his arms and put him outside the door in the street.

Kate quickly opened the cupboard door and pushed the piece of uniform at Mr. Lambert.

"Sorry," the soldier mouthed.

Kate took the dirty apron she'd put away in there earlier and closed the door. Her heart still hadn't slowed down! And now she could hear Liberty whimpering outside the apothecary door. She hated to have her dog shut out in the street—but she knew Colin was right. Without meaning to, Liberty could give them all away.

Suddenly, she was tired of the whole thing. She wished there was no deserter in the cupboard, no redcoats in the library, and that everything was the way it had always been. Being a spy no longer seemed exciting or brave.

When will all this be over? she wondered. *Will things ever go back to normal?*

Her mother stuck her head in the door of the apothecary, and both Kate and Colin jumped.

Mama laughed. "My, you two are as nervous as cats tonight." She looked down at the dirty apron Kate still clutched in her arms. "Take care of that, Kate, and put on a clean apron so you can help me put the food on the table. Supper is almost ready, and the officers are eager for their meal." Mama smiled at Colin. "You'll stay and eat with us, won't you, Colin?"

Colin hesitated. Kate was sure that he must be trying to keep his eyes from wandering toward the cupboard, just like she was. "Yes, ma'am," he said finally, and Kate was grateful that he wasn't going to leave her.

"Goodness," Mama said, cocking her head at the door. "Why is that dog shut out in the street? Let him in, Kate, and come along."

Mama disappeared again, and Kate looked at Colin. "You take care of Liberty," she whispered. "I have to help Mama. Maybe I can find a bone in the kitchen. If I can, I'll get it to you somehow. And then you can shut Liberty up in my room. He'll be quiet if he has a bone to gnaw on."

Smuggling a bone out from under Mama's eyes did not prove to be easy, though. Meanwhile, Kate could hear Liberty woofing and whining as he tried to figure out why such an interesting and un-usual scent was coming from the apothecary cupboard.

"What ails that dog?" Mama asked as she dished up the potatoes.

"Can't you quiet that dog?" Lieutenant Rand bellowed from the library.

In desperation, Kate held up the old stew bone she had found in the larder. "Can't I give this to Liberty, Mama? Then he'll be quiet and won't bother the officers."

Mama pushed a wisp of hair out of her face. She looked tired and worried, Kate noticed. "That's a good idea, Kate," Mama said absently. Kate gave a sigh of relief and hurried to take the bone to Colin.

At least the herbs must have worked, she thought an hour later. The officers ended their evening far earlier than usual. Stretching and yawning, they said good night. Those who boarded elsewhere headed out into the dark streets, while the others climbed the stairs to their rooms.

"Everyone seems tired today," Mama said with a long weary sigh. "I hope your father will be able to come home soon. He must be tired as well."

"Let me clean up," Kate said. "You go on up to bed."

Her mother gave a small, surprised smile. "Why, thank you, Kate. If you don't mind, I think perhaps I will retire early. If your father comes home before you go to bed, please tell him his supper is in the kettle over the fire." She smiled at both children. "Good night, Colin. Good night, Kate."

Kate and Colin looked at each other. At the same time, they both let out a long breath, as though they had each been trying not to breathe all evening. They stood for a moment listening to the silent house, then tiptoed into the apothecary. Now they had to get Mr. Lambert on his way before Father came home.

Colin shuttered the apothecary windows and barred the door so no one could surprise them. Then he opened the cupboard door. Kate turned her back so Mr. Lambert could slip quickly out of his uniform to change into his "new" clothes.

Colin chuckled. "Hope you don't mind looking like a woman."

Mr. Lambert grinned. "Not if it gets me out of Boston safely."

Colin helped Mr. Lambert into an old dress and petticoat of his mother's. A wig hid the man's brown curls. A lace-edged mobcap topped it all off. Kate bit back her giggles as she stuffed the uniform into the cloth bag and hid it behind some pottery in another cupboard.

Mr. Lambert shaved carefully with Harry's razor. He put on an old hooded cloak, slid a market basket Colin had brought over his

97

arm, and slipped into the dark street.

Kate knew Mr. Lambert was to meet a Patriot farmer who would be driving a cart a few streets over on his way home. Would Mr. Lambert make it? Or would the redcoats stop the funny-looking woman?

The next day, Kate heard Captain Ingles ask Colin about Mr. Lambert. "Did Lambert say where he was going when he left the apothecary?"

Colin shrugged. "Maybe he went to one of the taverns that are so popular with soldiers."

Kate grinned. At least she knew the man was still free! She was glad she'd buried the uniform in the herb garden early that morning.

Days later Harry said to Kate and Colin, "The post rider says the package you sent arrived safely."

Colin frowned. "The package?"

Harrison grinned, nodded, and walked away.

"Oh!" Kate's eyes met Colin's and they both grinned. The package was Mr. Lambert. If he "arrived safely," he must have made it out of Boston.

Kate wondered where he was living. Would he stay in another town in Massachusetts or on a farm, or would he live in another colony, far away from the redcoats that might recognize him? Would they ever see each other again?

CHAPTER 13

Fighting Friends and a Late-Night Secret

Colin and Kate spent fall days in the medical garden, removing plants before they were killed by early winter frosts. In the apothecary, they tied the plants together in bunches and hung them upside down from the ceiling to dry. Soon the ceiling was covered with fragrant purple, yellow, and white flowers.

One morning while Colin and Kate were tying up bunches of lavender thistle, the bell above the door jingled cheerfully, and Kate's friend Sarah entered.

Kate's face brightened. "Hello! I haven't seen you in days!"

"I've been busy." Sarah fumbled with the red-and-white-checked material covering the basket on her arm.

Kate nodded. "Me, too. We've been cleaning the garden. Tomorrow I'm delivering food baskets to some invalids and older ladies for the Gifts Committee. Will you help me?"

Sarah shook her head, her brown curls bouncing on the white linen scarf tied over the top of her blue dress. "I don't think so."

"But it would be fun! It would give us time to be together."

Sarah lifted her head with a jerk. Her blue eyes flashed. "I said no!"

Kate gasped and stepped back.

Sarah hurried to the counter and set down her basket. "I need some medicine. Mother's teeth are hurting." Her chin lifted and she glared at Colin. "We can't pay for it right now, but Father says to tell the doctor he'll pay for it as soon as the port opens again."

Colin nodded, pretending it was normal for Sarah's father to ask for credit. "Of course."

"I'll get the herbs." Kate took down a white china jar from a shelf.

"Is that the right medicine?" Sarah asked Colin.

"Yes," Colin assured her. "Kate's learned a lot about herbs from her father. If women could be doctors, she'd make a good doctor one day."

Kate spooned a bit of herb onto a piece of paper. Then she folded the paper so none of the herb could fall out and tied a bit of string about it. She handed the packet to Sarah. "Pour hot water over these herbs, the same as if you were making tea. Then have your mother put the wet leaves on her teeth."

"Thank you," Sarah mumbled, dropping the package into her basket. She hurried toward the door.

Kate shot Colin a worried glance. "Wait, Sarah, please." Kate bit her bottom lip, not sure what she should say next. "I don't know what I've done to make you mad," she said finally, "but I'm sorry."

Sarah started to walk around her without saying anything.

Kate grabbed her arm. "Please, Sarah, tell me what's wrong."

"It's the Gifts Committee you help with. My family is using some of the food and firewood people have donated. I'm so. . .ashamed." Tears ran down Sarah's freckled cheeks.

Kate stared at her, openmouthed.

Colin cleared his throat. "It's not your father's fault the king took away his job when the harbor closed. All the Patriots have to stick together and help each other through these hard times."

"Right now your family needs things other people can give them,"

Kate said. "Another time, your family will be helping someone. That's the way it works."

Sarah blinked at her tears. "When the tea was thrown into the harbor and later when the port was closed and the Patriots were all saying they'd starve before they'd pay for the tea, it felt so brave to be a Patriot." She brushed a hand over her eyes and sniffed. "It doesn't feel brave when you're begging for food."

Kate rubbed a hand on Sarah's arm. She wished she could make her friend feel better.

Sarah jerked away from Kate's touch. "It's Loyalists like your family who have made so much trouble for Boston."

"But Mama and Father didn't throw the tea in the harbor!"

"They didn't stand up with us, either." Sarah's voice jerked angrily. "If the Loyalists had stood by the Patriots, everything would have been fine. The king wouldn't have shut the harbor if everyone stood up to him together."

Kate stared at her. "Sarah, that's silly. You can't know what would have happened. No one can. Everyone has to do whatever they believe is right. That's what Father says."

Sarah sniffed. "I don't care what your father says. He's a Loyalist, and it's his fault everything is so terrible!" She sounded as though she might cry, but she held her head high and glared at Kate. "I don't want to be friends with you anymore, Kate Milton. I only want Patriots for friends." Sarah stormed out the door.

Kate turned to Colin. "I wish I could tell her," she whispered. "Maybe she wouldn't be so mad at me if she knew I was helping the Patriot cause."

Colin shook his head. "You know you can't tell anyone. The redcoats have to believe you're a Loyalist just like your parents. Then they'll never suspect you."

Kate frowned. "Sarah isn't right, is she? It's not the Loyalists' fault."

"No, it's not their fault. She's just hurting and doesn't know what to do about it."

Kate blinked away tears. "Well, hurting me won't help."

"No." Colin put his hand on her shoulder, then went back to his work.

Kate looked around the room. In all the jars of herbs, was there anything that would heal the wounds she and Sarah were feeling in their hearts? Was there any medicine for a broken friendship?

November moved into December. Days went along like usual until one evening during the second week of December, when Colin was again staying late at the apothecary shop while the officers played cards, smoked their long pipes, and visited.

Kate and Colin were trying to read a new medical book by candlelight, but Kate's eyes kept closing. Mama was already sleeping, and Father had sent word that he was delivering a baby and likely wouldn't be home until morning. Kate wished the redcoats would leave so Colin could go home to bed. Then she wouldn't feel guilty going to bed herself.

Suddenly, she heard words that wakened her like a clap of thunder: "Fort Harrison and Mary."

She nudged Colin. "Did you hear that?"

He nodded. On tiptoe, they moved to the closed library door and leaned their ears against it. Kate held her breath so she could hear better. What she heard set her mind whirling. British troops were being sent from Boston to Fort Harrison and Mary in New Hampshire!

"Harrison and the Observers need this news right away!" Colin whispered. He took one step toward the front door, but Kate grabbed his arm.

"You can't leave yet!" she hissed. "The officers might suspect something."

Chairs scraping against the library floor sent them dashing back to their chairs. Kate dropped her head and arms on the table and closed her eyes. After a moment, Colin pretended to be asleep, too.

Officers filed into the room, joking with each other. Kate's heart raced. Beside her, Colin was breathing as hard as if he'd just raced back from the Neck. She nudged him and made herself breathe slowly and deeply, as if she were sleeping.

Boots stopped beside the table. "Time to wake up, lad."

Colin blinked, sat up, and looked at the officers. He stretched his arms over his head. "Leaving?"

"Yes, lad," Captain Ingles answered. "Ye'd best see to banking the fireplace."

Colin pretended to yawn. "See you tomorrow night."

He and Kate stumbled toward the library while the officers left. He made quick work of banking the fireplace, while Kate snuffed the candles. Even with such an important message to deliver, they didn't dare leave the fire and candles burning.

"I'm going," Colin said, throwing his wool jacket around his shoulders.

Kate grabbed her cloak, as well. "I'm coming, too!"

Colin frowned at her and shook his head, but Kate knew he didn't want to take the time to argue.

Snow and ice made it hard to hurry along the dark, narrow streets. Only the moon and stars lit their way. A lantern might have been seen by soldiers or others. They didn't want anyone to remember seeing them on the street so late at night. Not when they were carrying an important Patriot secret!

Colin's house was dark and quiet when they reached it. The family was already in bed. Colin lit the candle on the hall table and carried it with them so he wouldn't fall and make noise. They didn't want to wake Lieutenant Andrews or Lieutenant Rand!

Kate's mind kept saying, *Hurry! Hurry!* but she walked slowly. She tried to remember which steps and which floorboards squeaked.

Creak! She and Colin froze. Kate's heart slammed against her chest. She wasn't as familiar with the creaks and squeaks in Colin's house as she was with her own. Had anyone heard her?

No one stirred. Colin slowly opened Harry's door.

While Colin shook Harry's shoulder, Kate held the candle high so Harry could see who it was. She put her finger to her lips.

Colin whispered in Harry's ear that he had news he must tell him right away.

"Kitchen," Harry whispered back.

Together they went downstairs, stepping over the squeaky places. This time, Kate was as silent as Colin. When they reached the kitchen, Harry opened the barrel of apple cider beside the back door. Taking the tin ladle hanging on the wall, he dipped the cool cider into three pewter mugs.

He handed mugs to Kate and Colin. "If anyone walks in, we'll say I woke up thirsty. I came down for a drink and met you two coming in." He cocked an eyebrow at Kate. "I take it you're spending the night with Susanna?"

"That's right." Kate felt guilty now that she had insisted on coming with Colin. If they were discovered, her presence might look odd to the officers. And if Mama woke up and found her gone, she would worry.

"I know you said we aren't to tell Patriot news in the house," Colin whispered, "but this is too important to wait until morning."

They stood close together beside the fireplace, where they could still feel a little heat from the banked ashes. Kate shivered at the eerie sound their whispers made in the large, dark room.

"What's your news?" Harrison asked.

Colin told how they'd overheard the officers. "General Gage is sending redcoats from Boston to Fort Harrison and Mary at Portsmouth, New Hampshire. They'll go by sea."

"Why?"

"There's only a few redcoats at the fort. General Gage wants more soldiers there in case the minutemen try to take the fort's gunpowder."

In the light of the candle Colin had set on the mantel, Kate could see excitement dancing in Harry's eyes. "The minutemen must get the gunpowder before the soldiers from Boston arrive."

"To do that, they'd have to go into the fort and take the powder from under the redcoats' noses," Colin said.

"Yes."

"But if the soldiers catch them, they might be shot."

"Yes," Harry agreed.

"I mean," Colin looked as though he were trying to put his worst fears into words, "if the redcoats and minutemen shoot at each other, war could start."

"Yes. Mark my words, if General Gage keeps taking Americans' guns and ammunition to use against us, war will surely start. If not at

Fort Harrison and Mary, then somewhere else."

Hopelessness filled Kate's heart. She didn't want war. She wanted peace with the king and his troops. She knew that most Patriots only wanted the king to listen to their complaints so that things would go back to being the way they had once been. That was all she wanted, too.

"If this news gets to the minutemen," Colin said slowly, "then Kate and I could start the war because it's our secret."

Harry's fingers squeezed Colin's shoulder tightly through the wool jacket. "This might be the most important news the Sons of Liberty have discovered. The Patriots must hear it."

"I thought the Continental Congress said the Patriots' army wasn't to shoot at the redcoats unless the redcoats shot first."

"That's right. But if the redcoats take all our ammunition, we won't be able to fight. We'll have to do whatever the king says, no matter how wrong it is."

Colin nodded slowly. Kate hadn't thought of that.

Harry rubbed a fist across his stubbly chin. "We need to tell Paul Revere. Portsmouth is sixty miles north, and the roads are covered with snow and ice. Paul's the only man we can count on to get through in time."

Kate saw Colin swallow hard. "Do. . .do you want me to tell him?"

Kate shivered. Would they have to sneak into Mr. Revere's house tonight?

Harry shook his head, his brown hair brushing his shoulders. "No, it's too dangerous. Even though you're only children, if you were caught entering Paul's house, the British might become suspicious. Mark my words, when they find the Portsmouth minutemen know the redcoats are being sent from Boston, General Gage will try to find how the news got out. We don't want anyone to remember you two from both Uncle Firth's house and Paul's the same night."

Colin yawned and picked up the wool blanket that was folded neatly at one end of the tall-backed settle. Kate yawned, too. Now that they'd passed the news and worry on to Harry, she was tired again. "I'm going to bed," Colin said, and Kate decided she would climb into bed with Susanna. She would be sure to wake up early in the morning so Mama would never know she was gone.

But Harry grabbed Colin's arm as he started to lay down on the settle. "Oh, no, you don't. You need to go back to Uncle Firth's and sleep in the library. That way the officers will find you there in the morning. No one must know you came home tonight. We don't want anyone to think you had a chance to tell Father and me what the officers said."

Colin sighed. Kate didn't want to go out in the cold and snow again any more than Colin did, but she knew Harry was right. They slipped quietly out the back door while Harry went to dress.

CHAPTER 14

The Raid

Harry got the message safely to Mr. Revere. Kate wondered what excuse Mr. Revere used to get out of town. General Gage didn't let people into or out of Boston without a pass anymore. To get a pass, you had to have a good reason to leave. Kate smiled at the thought of Paul Revere saying, "I'm off to warn the minutemen that you're sending soldiers to Fort Harrison and Mary." No, Mr. Revere would have come up with another reason.

Three days later, Colin told her Paul Revere was back. Kate was surprised he'd made the dangerous ride so quickly. Every day he was gone, Kate had prayed that Mr. Revere would be safe, the message would get through, and war wouldn't start.

Mr. Revere told Harry what happened at Fort Harrison and Mary. Harry and Uncle Jack printed the news in the *Boston Observer*.

Paul Revere had reached the minutemen before the soldiers from Boston arrived at the fort. In the middle of the night, the minutemen went to the fort in Portsmouth Harbor in boats. The British captain in charge of the fort fired three times at the minutemen, but he hit no one. The captain knew he didn't have enough soldiers at the fort to win a battle, so he surrendered.

Patriots, Loyalists, and redcoats in Boston were all shocked when they heard the news. Minutemen had taken a British fort without anyone on either side being wounded or killed!

Harry grinned when he told Colin and Kate the news. "The min-utemen carried away ninety-seven kegs of gunpowder and about one hundred guns and hid them. The minutemen need those guns and ammunition. They wouldn't have them without you two."

Kate couldn't help but be proud as she heard the town talk about the minutemen's raid. Lieutenant Rand and Lieutenant Andrews told the family that General Gage was mad that news of his plans had leaked out.

Mr. Revere made Colin and Kate gifts: small silver whistles shaped like spy glasses with the words "Boston Observer" carved on their sides. Kate carried hers with her everywhere. She would stick her hand in her apron pocket, feel the satiny smooth silver, and smile at the memory of Mr. Revere's and Harry's praises.

Kate's parents didn't like the news about Fort Harrison and Mary one bit. Mama was at the apothecary when Colin told them what had happened at the fort—without telling his and Kate's part in it, of course. Mama set the blue bottle she was dusting back on the shelf with a thud. "The minutemen must have known General Gage was sending soldiers to the fort." Her lips were pressed tight with disapproval.

"I suppose so," Father agreed.

Kate was checking the wooden medicine box Father kept in the trunk on the back of his carriage. It was her chore to keep the box stocked with twine, splints, bandages, sponges, medicines, and things to make pills and powders. She kept her eyes on her work, afraid to look up at her parents' faces.

The feathers in Mama's duster fluttered over a row of large jars with curving blue letters. "A spy must have told them."

Kate's heart lurched against her chest. She opened her mouth, but she couldn't say anything.

"Maybe one of his own soldiers," Mama continued. "I think it's awful, a British soldier betraying his country."

"Maybe it wasn't a soldier," Father said. "Maybe it was a Patriot who overheard the plans."

Kate glanced up quickly at her father, but he seemed absorbed with the medicine he was measuring.

Mama picked up a small metal scale in one hand, dusted the cupboard beneath it, and slammed it back down with a crash. "Citizens shouldn't betray their country, either," she snapped. "I'm just so tired of this terrible—" Her voice caught, and she broke off without finishing the sentence.

"Surely whoever told thought it was the right thing to do." Father's voice was grave.

"People like Jack and all the other Patriots always think they're doing the right things. But look what a mess they've made of Boston and of our lives!"

Colin shifted his shoulders uncomfortably. "They haven't done anything but ask the king to put things between England and the colonies back the way they were years ago, before the Stamp Act and the Tea Act, and—"

"They haven't done anything?" his aunt interrupted him, her voice shrill. "They've done everything! It's because of them the harbor is closed. I'm tired of making do with whatever food we can get. I want sugar and molasses instead of dried pumpkin for baking. I want new clothes for my family." She snatched up Kate's quilted skirt between her thumb and forefinger. "Look at this old thing! I've mended a dozen holes in it this winter, and it's too short for her. I'd be able to buy Kate a new dress if the port opened."

"But dear—" Father tried to hush his wife, but for once Mama wouldn't listen to him.

"I'm tired of sharing my house with strangers, too. I'm tired of our families arguing. Remember the good times our families used to have together? Now you and your brother-in-law don't even talk to each other!"

Father's lips curled just a little. "That's not the Patriots' fault, dear."

"Everything is the Patriots' fault!" She stamped her small slippered foot on the wooden floor. Kate had never seen her mother so upset.

"But, Mama," Kate said, "even Father says the king is punishing Boston more than is fair."

"I don't care. If I knew who the spy was that told General Gage's plans for Fort Harrison and Mary, I'd turn him in myself."

The marble pestle Colin had been holding hit the countertop and rolled onto the floor.

Father looked down thoughtfully at the pestle that had landed by his feet. Then he turned back to his wife. "You don't mean that. The spy could be someone you know, maybe even someone you care about."

Mama picked up the pestle and slammed it down on the counter. Her blue eyes were almost black with anger. "Spies make things worse. I want life to go back to the way it used to be."

"Turning against our neighbors isn't the answer."

Mama tugged at her lace-trimmed mobcap. "You call yourself a Patriot," she said to Colin, "but I know you also believe in doing what's right. Wouldn't you turn in a spy?"

"Maybe not, if he was someone I knew."

Mama threw up her hands in exasperation. "You're just as stubborn as your father, Colin Lang! You may not have joined the rebels who threw the tea in the harbor, but you're a Patriot just the same. Can't you see that all of you Patriots are hurting Boston?"

"I don't believe that," Colin said softly. Kate knew her mother's sharp words had upset him. Still, his voice sounded calm and reasonable.

But Kate knew her mother had refused to listen to reason.

Feelings grew worse between the redcoats and Patriots during the winter. The redcoats were afraid the Charles River would freeze over and that the minutemen would cross the ice to attack the troops.

But the river didn't freeze over. It was a mild winter, which was good for everyone in Boston. Fuel was scarce. A colder winter would have meant the poor people would have suffered more. The Patriots were sure God made the winter mild to help them.

Hopes for peace grew dimmer. The Patriots were preparing more and more for war. Patriot gunmakers were busy in all the colonies, making muskets for the minutemen. Paul Revere and other silversmiths made bullet molds. Colin's mother, Harry's wife, and other Patriot women gave their silver and pewter dishes and candlesticks to be melted down and made into bullets. Kate wondered if Lieutenant Andrews and Lieutenant Rand noticed the dishes and candlesticks missing from the house.

Larry came to town often, bringing things to market. He always stopped by to visit Colin and Kate. He told them how he and his father spent their evenings in front of the family fireplace carving wooden bowls and spoons the minutemen would need if war came.

Kate was glad there had been no fighting between the redcoats and minutemen. So far, the only people killed had been British deserters who had been caught and shot at the common. Each time it happened, Kate thought of Mr. Lambert. Where was he? Was he safe?

In February, General Gage's men tried to take the ammunition stored at Salem. Harry told Colin and Kate that Mr. Lambert, the deserter they'd helped escape, was living near Salem. He was helping train the minutemen.

The Observers hadn't been able to get a message to Salem. General Gage had locked Paul Revere, Harry, and some of their friends in jail at the fort on Castle Island to keep them from telling Salem. So now the Observers knew that the general had his own spy in the Observers.

Even without the Observers, Gage's men weren't able to take Salem's ammunition.

March fifth was the fifth anniversary of the Boston Massacre. People gathered at Old South Church to remember those who'd lost their lives at the hands of British soldiers. The building was packed. People were crushed together in the pews. The aisles were filled. Men even stood on the two-foot-deep windowsills. Kate knew the streets were crowded, too. Thousands had turned out.

Kate went with Colin and his family, but when she glanced up at the balcony, she saw that her parents were there, too. They sat where young Josiah Quincy had been the night of the tea party. Kate could still remember his chilling words that night:

"I see the clouds which now rise thick and fast upon our horizon. . .to that God who rides the whirlwind and directs the storm I commit my country."

Kate wondered, *How close is the storm of war now?*

Colin nudged her elbow and pointed toward the front of the

church. Kate almost laughed out loud when she saw Dr. Warren, the Patriot leader, climb into the church through the window above the high pulpit! He hadn't been able to make it through the crowd.

Dr. Warren was the one who had written the Suffolk Resolves that Colin and Harry had printed and Paul Revere had carried to the Continental Congress at Philadelphia last summer. Dr. Warren had come to the print shop to thank Colin's father for doing such a quick, good print job.

Wealthy John Hancock, who had been the leader of the Continental Congress, and Sam Adams, one of the smartest Patriot leaders, were beside Dr. Warren.

Forty British officers took the best pews at the front of the church and sat on the steps that led to the high pulpit. Colin and Kate exchanged worried glances. There was a rumor that General Gage was going to arrest the Patriot leaders today. The Loyalists had even made up a song about hanging them.

The redcoats couldn't frighten the Patriot leaders from speaking. Dr. Warren told the story of the Boston Massacre. He reminded the people of all the reasons they were proud to be English citizens.

"It isn't our aim to become a separate country from Great Britain," he said. "Our wish is that Britain and the colonies grow stronger together. But if our peaceful attempts aren't successful and the only way to safety lies through war, I know you will not turn your faces from the enemy."

The soldiers jeered. The crowd cheered. But no one was arrested at the meeting after all. Was it because the soldiers were afraid the crowd would turn on the redcoats if they arrested the popular leaders? Kate thought the leaders must have been frightened, even though they weren't arrested.

Out in the street after the meeting, Kate hurried to join her parents. The crowd about them parted to let Sam Adams and John Hancock through. Kate saw her mother's icy blue glare as the men walked past. Kate knew Mama hadn't changed her mind about Patriots.

In the days that followed, the Patriot leaders quietly slipped out of town, one by one, until only Dr. Warren was left.

The thunder of war sounded louder than ever.

CHAPTER 15
Danger

Kate smiled as she entered the printing shop. Spring had come at last, and the air outside was filled with the chatter of birds and the smell of cherry blossoms. The shop still smelled like ink. Uncle Jack always said ink was his favorite smell because ink printed words, and words were man's most powerful tools, next to faith in God.

Harry, Colin, and Uncle Jack looked up from their work and said hello. Colin handed her a freshly printed newspaper. "Read what Patrick Henry said."

Kate read it aloud.

> " 'We have done everything that could be done to stop the storm from coming. There is no longer any room for hope of peace. If we want to keep those rights for which we've been struggling for ten long years, we must fight!
>
> We shall not fight our battles alone. There is a just God, who rules nations. He will raise up friends to fight our battles for us.
>
> Is life so dear or peace so sweet as to be bought at the price of slavery? Forbid it, Almighty God. I know not what course others may take, but as for me, give me liberty or give me death!' "

Prickles ran up and down Kate's spine. The words filled her with a tingly sense of awe. She would always remember these words, she promised herself, and one day she would repeat them to her children. Still, she wondered how Patrick Henry could be so certain. Was it really so bad to live under Britain's rule? She was fairly sure she would never choose to die, no matter how unfair Britain's taxes might be.

"Do you think he's right?" she asked her uncle. "Do you think we'll have to fight?"

Uncle Jack looked very serious. "I think he's right."

Harrison nodded as well.

Kate and Colin walked outside. The sun still shone, warming the cobblestones. Redcoats, tradesmen, and housewives coming from market still filled the street. Idle craftsmen still sat on barrels and benches, visiting. Birds still chattered and cherry blossoms still perfumed the air.

But nothing was the same.

The next day, Kate saw people all over town reading the *Boston Observer* and heard them repeating Patrick Henry's words. In the afternoon, when Father said they could go, she and Colin hurried to Uncle Jack's shop with Liberty at their heels. They'd just arrived when a clattering in the street drew everyone to the door. Kate couldn't believe what she saw.

Lieutenant Rand and three other officers were riding their horses through the street. A large group of soldiers followed on foot, calling insults at the Patriots and laughing. Rand carried a large straw man. There was a grin on the lieutenant's face that made Kate's skin crawl.

People in the street hurried to get out of the horses' paths. Then they stopped and watched to see where the soldiers were going. Everyone knew what the straw man was for.

So did Kate. She'd seen others like it often enough.

As the officers pulled their horses to a stop in front of the shop, Rand leaped off his horse. He grinned at Colin and his father, then he and one of the other officers stopped a foot in front of them. Liberty growled deep in his throat, peeking at Rand from behind Kate's skirts. People in the street drew nearer, but Kate knew they couldn't stop the redcoats.

The other officer carried a rope with a noose at one end. He tossed the other end over the shop sign's metal pole, then hooked the noose over the straw man. Kate's stomach tightened when they pulled the straw man up, letting it swing in the breeze. She knew what they were doing. It was called hanging someone in effigy. They were pretending to hang Uncle Jack.

A copy of the *Boston Observer* was pinned to one straw hand. Rand grabbed a pipe from a nearby shopkeeper. He held it beneath the paper until it started on fire. Liberty yelped and scuttled away.

Colin darted into the shop. He grabbed the bucket of water that always stood beside the press. Kate knew the straw would go up like kindling and could start the building on fire. Water sloshed over the floor and Colin's shoes as he raced out the door with the bucket. The straw man was already one huge flame. The officers and his father had backed away.

Colin tossed the entire bucket on the burning form. Most of the fire went out in a hiss of smoke. The rope continued to burn, scorching the wooden shop sign.

Uncle Jack grabbed his composing stick, stuck it through the noose, and yanked the rope down. He stamped the flames out until only a smoking black circle remained.

Lieutenant Rand sat astride his bay horse and watched. Finally, he leaned over the horse's neck. "Patrick Henry may not be afraid of war, but you should be, Mr. Lang. If war breaks out, the treasonous printers will be among the first prisoners of war." He yanked at the reins, turned his horse, and galloped up the street, hooves clattering against the cobbles.

Colin's fists curled into balls. "I hate that man!"

His father's arm slid around his shoulders. "We're to love our enemies, Son. He needs our prayers, not our hate."

"Aren't we supposed to love everyone not just our enemies?" Colin asked.

"Yes, but it's hardest to be nice to our enemies."

"If that's true, why are you nicer to Lieutenant Rand than to Uncle Firth?" Colin stormed into the street, his wet shoes slapping against the cobblestones. Kate looked after him unhappily. She knew he wanted to be alone.

Kate was glad the next morning when her father asked her to work in the medical garden. It felt good to be outside in the sunlight with the birds singing and the smell of fresh earth. Her fear and anger over Lieutenant Rand's straw man lightened a little as she worked, pulling the tiny weeds that were growing around the young herbs.

The medical garden was more important than ever since the harbor had closed. Now when Father ran out of medicines and herbs, it was difficult and expensive to replace them unless he could get them from the garden. Kate sat back on her heels for a moment, enjoying the sunshine on her face, but she knew Mama would scold her if she came in with her face all red from the sun. She tightened the blue ribbons beneath her chin, pulling the sides of her huge round straw hat down over her cheeks.

Colin joined her in the garden and began turning the soft soil with a wooden rake. As they worked, the sound of fifes and drums playing a British march grew steadily louder, until it drowned out the songs of birds in the nearby trees. Colin and Kate moved to the white picket fence surrounding the garden to watch a regiment of redcoats parade past. Brass buttons and musket barrels flashed in the sun. Six young Patriot boys followed along singing "Yankee Doodle" at the top of their lungs.

"When the British troops first came to Boston, I thought everything would get better," Kate said. "Instead, everything got worse." She leaned against the fence. "Now, Sarah blames everything on the Loyalists—but I know that people like Mama and Father aren't to blame for everything that's wrong."

"Are you and Sarah friends again?"

She shook her head. "No. Sarah says she hates Loyalists and won't be friends with me anymore."

"I'm sorry, Kate."

"I always thought everything would work out between Britain and the colonies. But if Sarah can hate me because my parents are Loyalists and our fathers can stop talking to each other, maybe Britain and the colonies will stay angry, too. Maybe all this tension will never go away."

"Maybe."

Kate wrapped her fingers around the top of a picket in the fence and watched the troops disappearing down the street. "Everyone in Boston seems angry these days. People keep talking about war. Sometimes, Colin, I'm so scared."

He put a hand on her shoulder. The warmth of his hand comforted her, but she knew the thought of war scared him, too.

The next evening, Dr. Milton sent Colin to his father with a message to meet him after dark at the print shop. Colin exchanged looks with Kate, his brows raised in a silent question, but then he ran off to do what he was told.

Kate wanted to ask her father why he wanted to meet with Uncle Jack. Her curiosity made her feel both nervous and hopeful, all at the same time. His face was so grave, though, that she didn't dare ask him any questions.

The next morning, Father looked the same as ever as he went about opening the apothecary shop. Kate could hardly wait until Colin came. She was certain he would tell her what had happened.

Later, as they again worked in the garden, the children talked in excited whispers.

Colin, his father, and Harry had pretended to go to bed early the night before, Colin told Kate. They said good night to the family and officers. Then they sneaked out an upstairs window.

When they reached the print shop, Kate's father stepped out of a shadow and joined them. Uncle Jack made sure the wooden shutters were closed over the windows. Inside, Harry lit a single candle from a warm coal in the banked fireplace. In the wavering light of the candle, the three Langs faced Dr. Milton.

Colin's father crossed his arms over his chest. "You haven't spoken to me for six months, Firth. Now you order me and my sons to the print shop in the dark of night. Why?"

"General Gage is planning to take your press and arrest you for treason."

"No!" Colin yelled. He couldn't bear it to be true! His father and brother couldn't be arrested!

His father put his hand on Colin's shoulder. "Quiet, son. How do you know this, Firth?"

Dr. Milton hesitated a moment. "An officer I trust told me. He knows my sister is your wife."

"Why arrest us now?" Harrison asked.

"A ship arrived this week from England with a letter from the king to General Gage. The king told him to be tougher on the Patriots," Dr. Milton said. "You and your father need to leave town."

"Gage won't give us a pass out of town when he wants to arrest us," Uncle Jack said. "Maybe Harry or I could sneak out of town, but how could we sneak both our families out?"

Sweat trickled down Kate's spine as she listened to Colin's story. She remembered the deserter she and Colin had seen captured at the gate. Would that happen to Harry and Uncle Jack?

"Then your father said, 'I've been thinking about this for hours.' " Colin continued with his story.

"General Gage won't hurt your families," Kate's father had said. "It's you and Harry he wants. I promise to watch out for your families until you can return or they can join you. Because I'm a Loyalist doctor, I have a pass that lets me enter and leave Boston freely. The guards at the Neck see me so often that they don't even search me. I can sneak you out in my carriage."

Harry grinned. "That's a great idea!"

Relief poured through Kate as she listened. It was the perfect plan! She felt so proud of her father. No matter what he believed, he would always stand by the people he loved.

Colin shook his head when he saw Kate's excited face. "My father said, 'No.' "

Uncle Jack had shaken his head and crossed his arms over his large chest. "I won't let you put yourself in danger. The officers at our house would quickly find we'd left town. When they found you'd left town the same night, you'd be arrested."

Dr. Milton's arms had swung wide. "What else can you do?"

"We can find a way out of Boston ourselves." Uncle Jack raised his eyebrows and looked at Harry. "Can't we?"

Colin knew he was asking Harry whether he could get them out the same way Harry had helped other deserters out of Boston.

Harry nodded. "We'll find a way."

"If you can't find another way out," Dr. Milton said, "promise you'll let me help you."

"I promise. I'll never forget this, Firth, not the warning or the offer to put yourself in danger to help us."

Colin had thought the candlelight reflected off unshed tears in his father's eyes. A moment later he'd decided he must have been wrong. He'd never seen his father cry.

Uncle Jack cleared his throat. "Colin said something to me yesterday that's been bothering me ever since."

Colin had looked at him in surprise. What had he said?

"He said he didn't understand why we were nicer to our enemies than to you, Firth." Colin's father held out his huge, ink-stained hand. "Our families have worked together down through the years. I'd like us to be friends, in spite of our differences. I'm asking you to forgive me."

Slowly, Kate's father took his brother-in-law's hand. "And I as well."

"You told me often that God says we're to pray for our leaders," Uncle Jack said. "Maybe that's a good place to start over."

"For King George?" Kate's father asked.

"Yes—and the Patriot leaders."

"Oh, all right." Dr. Milton had grinned. "I guess they can all use the Lord's help. I only hope it's not too late for peace."

"If war comes," Harry said, "the leaders of both sides will need the Lord's help more than ever."

The four joined hands in the middle of the dark room. They prayed for wisdom for King George and the Patriot leaders and for peace in America.

After Kate's father left, Uncle Jack had put a hand on each of his sons' shoulders. "We've printed only what we believed was right. We have to trust that God will make a way of escape for us."

Harry had left to talk to friends in the Sons of Liberty who could help them find that way of escape. Colin and his father began taking apart the press. "We make our living by it," Uncle Jack said. "We can't let it be destroyed." He knew friends who would hide the press in their cellar.

Kate blinked tears from her eyes as Colin finished his story. "What will your family do now?"

Colin shrugged. "Father told me to come to work here just as though everything was normal. We're waiting for Harry to tell us what to do next."

Only an hour later, Harry stopped by the apothecary shop. The Langs' escape was arranged. "Tomorrow is Easter Sunday," Harry reminded them. "The soldiers won't dare arrest us until after church. That will give Father and me time to say good-bye to our families."

Kate looked at Harry. "You have to leave?" She already knew the answer. Would baby Paul remember his father when he grew up? Kate could not hold back the tears that filled her eyes.

After church the next day, Harry told the other family members and Lieutenant Andrews, who always joined them for services, that he and his father wanted to check something at the shop before Sunday dinner.

"See you at dinner," Uncle Jack said. He smiled at Kate's parents. "You and Kate will join us, won't you?"

The Miltons nodded and smiled. "We'll see you later," Father said, his voice calm and sure.

Kate watched as Colin and his mother and sisters walked home. They were chatting and laughing as they walked, as though inside their hearts weren't breaking with fear and sadness. They didn't want Lieutenant Andrews or anyone else to see how frightened they were.

Would Harrison and Uncle Jack escape? When would their family be together again?

Kate prayed all the way home.

CHAPTER 16

A Mission of Mercy

By Tuesday evening, Colin and his family still hadn't heard whether his father and Harry were safe. "They must be," Colin told Kate. "If they'd been caught, the soldiers would have told us."

Kate was certain Lieutenant Rand would have loved to have given the bad news. The officer had been furious when he'd found the two Lang men had left town. *He must have known General Gage was planning to arrest them,* Kate thought.

A few days later, when Kate and Colin stepped through the front door of his home, they heard a man's voice they didn't recognize coming through the closed sitting room door. The next voice they did know: Lieutenant Rand's. They silently exchanged looks, then leaned their ears against the door to listen.

The voice they didn't know was speaking now. "You and Lieutenant Andrews are to report to the common as soon as possible, prepared for an expedition."

"Lieutenant Andrews isn't here," Lieutenant Rand said, "but I'll get the message to him."

Kate and Colin stepped quickly from the doorway. Opening the front door, Colin pretended they were just entering the house as Lieutenant Rand and a soldier came out of the sitting room.

The soldier nodded at the children and left. Lieutenant Rand frowned at Colin. "Do you know where Lieutenant Andrews is?"

"I haven't seen him, sir."

Rand grabbed his hat from the hallway table. "I'm going looking for him. If he gets back before I do, tell him to wait for me here."

Kate watched Rand hurry down the street in his red coat and black hat. The officers were to be "prepared for an expedition," the soldier had said. That meant General Gage was sending his soldiers out of Boston, likely to take another town's gunpowder. *We should tell Paul Revere*, Kate thought, *but how many men is Gage sending and where?*

Kate and Colin worried about it for fifteen minutes, pacing back and forth in front of the fireplace, talking in whispers. They could hear women's voices in the kitchen, and Kate knew Colin's mother and sisters must be making supper. "Should we ask your mother?" she whispered.

Colin shook his head. "I have to figure out what to do." All of a sudden, he sounded more like a man than a boy.

When Lieutenant Andrews walked in, Susanna was with him. Her hand was tucked into the crook of his elbow.

"Lieutenant Rand is looking for you, sir," Colin said.

Kate almost blurted out that he was to go to the common, but she remembered just in time that she wasn't supposed to know that!

Lieutenant Andrews didn't answer. Instead, he looked at Susanna. Their faces were filled with worry. The officer removed his hat and turned to Colin. "While we were walking by the common, an officer stopped us. I'm to report there right away."

So he'd already heard the message.

Susanna said, "Boats are waiting by the common to take soldiers across the river." She glanced at Lieutenant Andrews and back to Colin. "It's not a secret. Anyone from town who goes to the common can see what's happening."

"Is it a secret where the troops are going?" Colin asked.

"Yes." Lieutenant Andrews played with his hat and bit the corner of his bottom lip as if he couldn't decide whether to say more.

"They're going to try to take more of our ammunition, I suppose," Colin said.

Lieutenant Andrews took Susanna's hand. "When I came to America, I expected only to follow my orders and serve the king. I didn't expect to meet Susanna or find I agree with the Patriots' beliefs. I didn't think I would ever betray my king and fellow soldiers, but to do otherwise would be to betray my conscience."

Kate waited for what he would say next, her heart beating faster and faster.

The officer took a deep breath. "It's rumored we're going to Concord, on the other side of Lexington. Maybe we are to take the Americans' arms there in obedience to King George's recent orders. You must warn the Sons of Liberty, Colin."

Colin ran out of the house with Kate right on his heels. They headed for Paul Revere's house. When they reached the house in North Square, Colin banged on the door.

Kate looked over her shoulder nervously. The streets were filled with redcoats dressed for battle. "Try not to look so upset," she hissed. She tried to laugh as she said the words so that the officers would think nothing of two children out paying a call. She knew many marines were quartered in nearby houses, including Major Pitcairn, one of the best-liked British officers—even by the Patriots.

Mr. Revere greeted them with the smile he always wore. "Young Lang. Mistress Milton. You must be here about the delivery. I heard only an hour ago that it arrived safely."

"Delivery?" Colin stared at him blankly. "Oh, the delivery!" Kate knew Mr. Revere must be speaking about Uncle Jack and Harry. They were safe! Joy and relief flooded her in spite of the hard news they carried.

"Thank you, sir, but that isn't why I'm here." Colin whispered Lieutenant Andrews's message.

Mr. Revere nodded. "I've heard the same from two other sources."

Kate was disappointed that Mr. Revere already knew their news.

"To hear it from more than one Observer only makes it more likely the news is true. It was brave of you to come. Tell no one else," Mr. Revere warned.

Would Mr. Revere ride again tonight for the Sons of Liberty? Kate wondered. If he did, he'd have to sneak past the soldiers at the Neck or the warships in the harbor.

If there was war, would Harry and the other minutemen face the officers who had been living in their homes? Lieutenant Andrews had shared his army's secret, but he hadn't said he would desert and become a Patriot. Could Andrews shoot at Harry or Harry at him?

Kate's stomach felt sick.

As the children headed back to Kate's house, they saw Dr. Milton's carriage leaving. To Kate's surprise, Larry was on a horse beside the carriage. "Uncle Firth!" Colin sprinted down the street after the carriage, and Kate struggled to keep up on her shorter legs.

Her father drew on the reins and looked down at the children. "Larry's father is ill," he said. "We're on our way out to their farm. I may need to operate. I could use your help, Colin."

"May I come, too?" Kate asked.

Her father hesitated. "Your mother may not want you to go."

"May I go ask?" she pleaded.

Her father nodded, and she dashed for the house. Her mother met her at the door.

Mama smiled as Kate fought to get the words out between her gasps for air. "Save your breath," she said. "I know what you're going to ask. And I've also come to realize how important healing is to you. So long as you stay with your father, you may go."

Kate gave her mother a grateful hug, then ran back to the carriage where Father, Colin, and Larry were waiting.

The wheels clattered over the cobblestones. Kate looked back. Her mother was still standing in front of the house, staring after them. Her face was lined with worry, and Kate suddenly realized how much courage it must take to be a parent and let your children grow up. Especially in dangerous times like these. Kate waved her hand at her mother, hoping Mama would know how much she loved her. Her mother's face lightened as she returned the wave, then turned to go back inside.

They stopped at Colin's house to let his mother know where they were going, and then they were on their way. "It would save us a lot of time if we could take the Charlestown ferry from the north end of Boston," Father grumbled. "Instead we have to go south across the Neck, then north. It will take us twice as long to get there. I hope the extra time won't cost Larry's father his life."

There was a moment at the Neck when Kate didn't think they'd be allowed to leave Boston. The guards had told Father that he and Kate could leave but not Colin or Larry. Dr. Milton convinced them that Larry's father was truly ill, that Larry was needed to show him the way to the farm, and that he needed Colin to assist him.

They'd been driving a long time when Kate looked across the river toward Boston. She could see campfires on the common and candlelit windows, but darkness pressed all around them. A lantern swung from each side of the carriage roof, helping light the way for the horses. The night sounds of owls, insects, and toads kept them company.

Colin pointed out two lights, higher than any others, to Dr. Milton and Kate. "Someone must have hung lanterns in the tower of Christ Church," he said. "Isn't that strange?"

CHAPTER 17
War!

When they arrived at the farmhouse, Dr. Milton grabbed his black bag. "Colin, help Larry with the horses. See that you're quick about it. Bring the medicine chest."

Kate had been worrying about something all the way from Boston. Mr. Revere had told them not to tell anyone else Lieutenant Andrews's secret, but the silversmith hadn't known she and Colin would be leaving town that night, traveling the very road the British would likely travel to reach Concord. He hadn't known Kate and Colin would be at a farmhouse just outside Lexington, the town the redcoats would have to pass through on their way.

Larry was helping Colin unhitch Dr. Milton's horses from the carriage. Kate took the opportunity to whisper into Colin's ear. Colin nodded, then took a deep breath, and turned to Larry. "Larry, can you get a message to the minutemen around here?"

Larry's hands froze on the reins. "Tonight?"

Colin nodded, darting a look over his shoulder at the farmhouse. Kate's father had already gone inside. Colin told Larry Lieutenant Andrews's secret while they took the horses to the barn to be fed, watered, and brushed down.

"Guess I'm not too surprised," Larry said. "This afternoon the minutemen were called to Lexington Green when British officers were spotted on the roads. When none of our lookouts saw troops coming, the men were sent home."

He grinned at Kate and Colin across the horse's back. "If the redcoats are figurin' to find any guns at Concord, they're goin' to be mightily disappointed."

"Why?"

"Paul Revere warned the Concord Patriots on Sunday that the redcoats were beginnin' to act a might suspicious, pullin' men off duty to train. Concord seemed the likely place for the redcoats to head. The Massachusetts Congress was meetin' there. Would've been easy for Gage's men to arrest all the most powerful Patriot leaders in Massachusetts. Then, too, it's the nearest place to Boston with a good supply of ammunition and guns."

"How do you find out so much, Larry?"

"Livin' in the country isn't like livin' in Boston. We don't have redcoats tellin' us what we can and can't do and livin' in our houses. We don't have to worry 'bout the redcoats overhearin' us if we talk 'bout Patriot doin's. Sunday I visited cousins in Concord. We had a grand time hidin' things."

"Hiding what things?"

"Ammunition and guns, of course." He snorted. "The redcoats will never find them. We dropped bags of bullets in the swamps, and we buried the cannons in a farmer's field."

Kate and Colin burst out laughing at the thought of a farmer plowing over cannons.

When the horses were cared for, Larry saddled his father's only other horse. Then he raced toward the house to check on his father. Soon he was back carrying an old squirrel gun.

"We'll stop those redcoats," he told the children. He swung

himself up onto his horse's back. "Thanks for the warnin', friends."

He was off. Would he warn the minutemen in time to truly stop the redcoats?

Father frowned at the children when they finally went inside. "I thought I told you to hurry." He didn't waste time with more scolding. Instead, he quickly told Colin what was wrong with Larry's father. He was going to operate, and Colin would need to help. "You can make yourself useful, as well, Kate, by handing me things as I need them."

Father took instruments from his black bag and laid them on the kitchen table, where he'd be operating. Kate pulled off her cloak and wrapped one of her father's black aprons over her dress to protect the blue homespun from getting spattered with blood.

The fireplace's heat warmed away the chill from their night ride. Like all kitchen fireplaces, it was as wide as she was tall and almost as high. Kate could smell cornmeal mush cooking slowly in the large black kettle hanging from a crane over the low flames. The smell reminded Kate that she hadn't eaten since noon, and her stomach growled. There was no time to think of food now, though.

Hours later, about two in the morning, when a horse's hooves were heard slamming against the dirt farm lane, Colin and Dr. Milton didn't even look up from their patient. Kate, however, was weary from holding the lantern high so that her father could see. Larry's mother took it from her hand to let her rest, and Kate stepped out onto the front porch to breathe the night air. A moment later, the hoofbeats drew nearer. With a thrill, Kate heard a man call, "The redcoats are coming! Patriots turn out!" Then the sound of hooves headed back down the lane.

When she stepped back inside, her father had paused in his work. In the light of the lantern, he looked across the wooden table at

Colin. Kate saw Colin look back at him without saying a word. Then they both went back to work. The redcoats and minutemen might be planning to meet, but Kate knew they both agreed that their duty now was to save the man in front of them.

Kate's head was starting to nod when a sharp noise startled her awake. Colin's head jerked up as well.

"Gunfire!" Father exclaimed. "The locals must be waking the countryside, letting them know the redcoats are coming."

Soon they heard a bell ringing. Larry's mother said it was the bell from a church at Lexington, another way to wake the people. Before long other church bells from nearby villages joined in. The gong of bells kept up all night.

Kate's father drew the last stitch at about four in the morning, closing the operation. Larry's father was still alive. Kate knew he was still in danger, though. Many people died from surgery because of infections.

Larry's mother gave them cornmeal mush for breakfast. To pay for the operation, she gave Dr. Milton a large smoked ham. Colin put it in the trunk the doctor kept on the back of his carriage, while Larry's mother wrapped in rags three stones she'd heated in the fireplace. Kate, Colin, and Father placed them at their feet in the carriage to ward off the cold morning air.

They were on the road before four-thirty. Dogs barked and howled. Church bells still sounded through the darkness. Candles lit farmhouse windows, and they weren't the only ones on the road. Men on foot and horseback were hurrying toward Lexington.

"Fools," Father muttered, slapping the reins against the horses' flanks. "Don't they know better than to anger the king's troops?"

Neither Kate nor Colin answered. Kate gripped the edge of the carriage seat, swaying as the horses moved along the rutted road only a little faster than a walk. They had sixteen miles back to Boston. Kate knew her father didn't want to tire the horses too soon.

When they neared Lexington Green, where Kate and Colin had watched the minutemen practice months before, the gray sky of dawn revealed the shadows of men in front of the meetinghouse. The road ran alongside the green, and beyond the meetinghouse, Kate saw a dark column moving closer, growing larger and larger. "Redcoats!" she whispered.

Father urged his horses to the side of the road, beneath a large tree beside a rock wall. They would have to wait until the redcoats passed to continue.

A drum began its *rat-a-tat-tat*. They heard the captain order the minutemen to fall in. The men formed two lines in front of the meetinghouse. There were only about seventy of them, Kate guessed— farmers and craftsmen from the way they were dressed. About forty townspeople looked on from doorways and windows and behind stone walls.

Was Larry with the minutemen? Kate wondered, leaning forward on the seat to see better in the dim light. The lanterns still swung from the carriage top, but they were no help any longer. Colin lifted the glass sides and blew out the candles.

Two men hurried behind the minutemen carrying a trunk. Kate recognized one of them: Paul Revere. So he'd made it out of Boston to warn the countryside after all. Maybe Larry's warning hadn't been needed.

"Let the redcoats pass. Don't fire unless you're fired upon!" the captain called to his men.

A moment later, the redcoats marched past the meetinghouse and onto the green. "There are a lot more redcoats than minutemen!" Colin said.

Father nodded grimly. "Even the most hotheaded rebel wouldn't be foolish enough to fight against such odds."

Colin nudged Kate and pointed out Major Pitcairn, who was quartered with Paul Revere's neighbors. He was one of the redcoats' leaders.

The redcoats stopped about 150 feet from the Patriots. Major Pitcairn rode up to the minutemen, his sword drawn. "Ye rebels, disperse! Lay down your arms! Why don't ye lay down your arms?"

There was a flash of gunpowder, the roar of a musket. Then another and another!

Colin leaped to his feet, setting the carriage rocking, but Kate cringed against her father's shoulder. She couldn't tell who had fired first. Now both sides were firing! Gunpowder smoke filled the air.

Some minutemen scurried away, dodging redcoats' musket balls and bayonets. Some hid behind trees and walls or headed toward nearby buildings. Others stayed where they were. The redcoats hurried after the minutemen. Bodies were falling from the musket fire! A minuteman not much older than Colin was hit in the chest with a musket ball. He crawled away, bleeding heavily. Kate knew she was going to be sick. Her father put his arm around her while she leaned out the carriage window.

Major Pitcairn whirled his horse around. His sword flashed as he brought it down in a motion Colin knew meant to stop firing. But the redcoats didn't stop firing! Minutemen shot from the green, from behind a stone wall, and from nearby buildings.

Horrified, Kate watched a redcoat jam the bayonet on the end of his musket into a fallen Patriot. Her stomach lurched again.

Major Pitcairn fell with his horse. Had the friendly officer been hit? Kate breathed a sigh of relief when the major stood. His horse had been hit, though.

A musket ball whizzed over the carriage, and Father yanked the children out of the carriage. "Get behind the stone wall!" he ordered. He followed them, keeping hold of the horses' reins, which wasn't easy. The bays tried to bolt, frightened by the muskets.

Minutemen raced to get away from the redcoats. Some fled down a road. Most crossed a swamp to reach safe land.

Only minutes had passed when the fighting ended. Kate's anger boiled over as the redcoats cheered. How could they cheer killing and hurting people? Their officers struggled to get the troops in order again. Only one or two redcoats had been wounded and none killed. Soon the cheerful troops set off down the road toward Concord.

Father grabbed his black leather bag. "We'd best see if we can help any of these foolish rebels."

The children followed him. Already some of the wounded were being carried to nearby homes and Buckman's Tavern. The man Kate had seen bayoneted was dead. So was the young man she'd seen crawling away. In all, eight men were dead. Kate was glad to see Larry wasn't among them. Nor was Larry one of the ten wounded.

Kate clung to her father's sleeve, trying her best not to be sick again. If she truly wanted to be a healer, she knew she could not let such sights frighten her. She had often helped her father treat patients with illnesses and broken bones. She'd seen her share of blood and dying. But she had never seen violence like this.

It's the wounded who are important, not me, she told herself again and again. She made herself watch carefully as her father used a steel probe to find musket balls, then used a bullet extractor—shaped much like scissors—to remove them. Someday, she told herself, she might have the opportunity to do this herself. After the musket balls were removed, Dr. Milton let Colin put plasters from the medicine box on the wounds. Then Kate bound them up with strips of material she ripped from her petticoats.

They were there for hours, first helping the wounded, then eating lunch at Buckman's Tavern. While at lunch, they were surprised when Colin's father and Harrison joined them, guns in their hands. They found out that Uncle Jack and Harry had been staying at a farm near Lexington since leaving Boston. The Langs had fought on Lexington Green!

Harry looked pale. "The man next to me was killed by the redcoats. He never fired a shot. One minute he was alive and the next he was dead. You were right, Colin, when you said it's easier to kill a man than to keep him alive."

Suddenly a man rushed in. "Redcoats are headed back this way! Concord's men are chasin' them! Patriots turn out!"

Harry and Uncle Jack grabbed their guns and jumped up. "We have to go," Uncle Jack said. "Tell your mother we're safe, Colin. We'll be in touch."

Kate's heart sank as they ran into the tavern hallway and out the front door. If they kept fighting, would they ever see them alive again?

Father pushed his chair back from the table. "We had best make ourselves useful, Colin." He looked at his daughter. "I want you to stay here, Kate. We'll bring the wounded back here, and you can help us then—but your mother would never forgive me if I didn't do my best to keep you out of harm's way."

Kate could tell from his face that there was no point arguing. Her heart racing, she watched from the tavern window as they rode away. Before long, they were back with the carriage full of wounded men.

After that, Kate was too busy to be afraid.

"Hello, Kate."

Kate looked up in surprise from the wound she was bandaging. The wounded man she knelt beside was Lieutenant Andrews! A musket ball had hit him in the thigh.

Lieutenant Andrews told them a bit of what happened at Concord. The town militia had treated them politely, escorting them into town with drums and fifes. But when Major Pitcairn ordered his men to destroy a bridge, fighting started.

When the redcoats headed back to Lexington along the tree-lined road, the minutemen and other colonials had kept up a constant fire. The redcoats had been sitting ducks in the middle of the road while the minutemen shot from behind trees, bushes, fences, and sometimes from houses.

"We didn't stand a chance," Lieutenant Andrews said, gritting his teeth against the pain as Dr. Milton removed the musket ball. "Many of our soldiers have been killed or wounded."

So the redcoats have "won" the battle on Lexington Green, Kate thought, *but the Patriots are "winning" the rest of the battle. The Patriot who had shot Lieutenant Andrews will never know that the officer had tried to help the Patriots by telling Colin and her the redcoats' plans,* Kate thought as Colin and her father moved on to another wounded man. The sound of musket fire and shouting continued while they worked.

"There will be no turning back now," Father said grimly late that afternoon as they were finally riding home.

Questions ran through Kate's mind. What would happen next? How many minutemen and redcoats would die or be maimed? What would happen between friends and families who were on opposite sides of the conflict? How would the redcoats treat Patriots in

Boston? Would the Patriots be safe?

The time Kate had dreaded for so long had come. She gripped the edge of the seat until her fingers hurt.

"It's a war now," Colin said softly. "Will I have to fight?"

Dr. Milton sighed. "Not yet. You're still a boy. But if the war lasts another year or two, it's very likely you'll be called on to fight. You'll be a man, after all."

Another year or two of fighting? Kate gasped at the words. Surely, it couldn't last that long!

"I'm not sure I'm ready."

Kate's father smiled a little. "To be a man or to fight? You've no choice in one and little in the other."

Colin lifted his chin. "If I have to fight, I'll have to carry a gun, but I want to carry a doctor's tools, too. Maybe I can be a doctor's helper for the army. Will you teach me all you can?"

"Me, too, Father?" Kate looked up into her father's face. "I can be useful." She had learned something today: Battlefields were places of killing, but they were places of saving lives, too. "Plenty of women are healers. You'll need all the help you can get."

Her father looked down at her. Then he sighed. "I'm afraid you're right, Kate. But I can make no promises now. I'm too weary. We need to get you home to your mother."

Kate leaned her head on her father's shoulder. The months ahead would be frightening ones, she knew. But everything she had seen today convinced her even more that she wanted to play her part.

I know I'm only a little girl, she thought sleepily, *but God, please make me useful.*

As her eyes sank shut, she was certain that one way or another, God would answer her prayer.

OFFICIAL

SISTERS IN TIME

WEBSITE!

Your Adventure Doesn't Stop Here—

LOG ON AND ENJOY...

The Characters:
Get to know your favorite characters even better.

Fun Stuff:
Have fun solving puzzles, playing games, and getting stumped with trivia questions.

Learning More:
Improve your vocabulary and knowledge of history.

Plus you'll find links to other history sites, previews of upcoming *Sisters in Time* titles, and more.

Don't miss
www.SistersInTime.com!

If you enjoyed

Kate
and the Spies

be sure to read other

SISTERS IN TIME

books from BARBOUR PUBLISHING

- Perfect for Girls Ages Eight to Twelve

- History and Faith in Intriguing Stories

- Lead Character Overcomes Personal Challenge

- Covers Seventeenth to Twentieth Centuries

- Collectible Series of Titles

6" x 8 ¼" / Paperback / 144 pages / $3.97

AVAILABLE WHEREVER CHRISTIAN BOOKS ARE SOLD.